The Ranger

The Ranger

A McAllister Brothers Romance

Julia Justiss

The Ranger

Tule Publishing First Printing, July 2021

The Tule Publishing, Inc.

First Publication by Tule Publishing 2021

Cover design by Lee Hyat Designs

ISBN: 978-1-954894-44-0

Dedication

To the Justiss Family of Morris County, Texas, who have for 170 years served their God, their family and their land.

Author's Note

Like my Navy pilot father-in-law, after retirement my Navy husband came back to buy property in Morris County, where his ancestors were among the first three settling families in the area. His grandfather, great and great-great-grandfathers farmed cotton, sorghum and sweet potatoes, planted fruit and nut trees, ran a syrup mill, operated a blacksmith shop, and dedicated their lives to improving their land and livestock. Marrying into this family, members of which still run the Justiss Ranch, inspired me to want to write a story about characters with equally deep ties to their family and their land.

Although the Texas location is slightly different—my story takes place in the Hill Country of central Texas, rather than the Piney Woods of northeast Texas—the love for the land and family is the same. I hope my McAllister Brothers stories will convey to readers that legacy of loyalty and devotion.

Chapter One

WITH A SATISFIED sigh, Brice McAllister finished the last of his take-out burger and leaned back in the Adirondack chair on the deck of his brother Grant's newly refurbished cabin, sipping a soda water and admiring the view across the Balcones hills and down to the narrow valley through which the creek ran.

"Got to admit, Great-Grandad chose a prime site to build his cabin," he said to his brother Duncan, who dropped his lean frame into a chair beside him. "Can see practically to three counties from here."

"Course, when he built it, there were still Comanche raids in the area as well as marauding outlaw bands," Duncan said. "He needed to be able to see to three counties to protect his family."

"I'm just glad Grant decided to redo the place. It's a showpiece."

"Credit my lovely wife," Grant said, coming out to join them. "The grunt labor of ripping out floors and walls, drywall, painting and finishing was mine, but the touches that make it so special are all her."

"She's a terrific designer," Duncan said. "The place is modern and comfortable, but it's still a cabin. Nothing frou-frou or cutesy, despite being furnished by a girl."

"Speaking of wives, did you married guys get a special dispensation from your better halves to allow you to meet for lunch here today? I mean, not that you can't come and go when you please," Brice said, adding a *bauk-bauk-bauk* chicken sound imitation.

"He's inferring we're henpecked," Duncan said to Grant.

"Nah, he's just jealous. Because we go home to two beautiful, hot, talented babes at night and he just has an empty condo in Austin," Grant replied. "So sad. Not even a dog to keep him company."

"Well, he's the youngest. He always was a little slow." Duncan grinned.

"If I weren't so comfortable in this chair, I'd get up and whup you," Brice said.

"You could try, but I wouldn't advise it," Grant said.

"Hmm . . . Recon Marine or Texas Ranger . . . which one would I put my money on?" Duncan mused.

"Enough brotherly mutual admiration," Brice said dryly. "I've just finished up a case and am cooling my heels, waiting to be summoned to testify at the trial, so I thought I'd rummage around and see if I can turn up anything on those harassment incidents you've told me about."

"I'd bet you anything Marshall Thomason is behind them," Duncan said.

"Just because the two of you have detested each other since high school isn't enough reason to put him under surveillance," Brice said.

"Maybe not, but something isn't right there," Duncan said. "Is it only coincidence that Harrison started having all sorts of problems—fence lines cut, brush damning up creeks—after she inherited the Triple A? With Thomason approaching her in his slick rich-boy way, commiserating on how hard it was for a city girl with no experience to try to carry on her daddy's ranch, and how he'd be happy to take it off her hands for a good price if she decided to go back to her accountant's job in Dallas?"

"And there have been more incidents since you two got hitched and reunited the two parts of the Triple A," Grant said. "Worst of which was losing Halsey."

Duncan shook his head. "Her father's prize herd bull, who was almost like a pet. She still hasn't gotten over the shock of finding him dead on the road after a gate was 'somehow' left open. Brice, you know none of us would leave a gate open, ever, especially not one near a road with blind curves and eighteen-wheeler traffic. We're just lucky the truck driver wasn't killed too."

"If it weren't for Grant's wife's great ideas about using the Scott Ranch house as a conference center, bringing in some additional income, we would be in a pretty difficult situation, losing Halsey's stud fees. We were counting on them for a lot of our operating cash over the next several years," Duncan said.

"Thomason's been nosing around all the ranchers, trying to get ones teetering on the brink of solvency to sell out," Grant added.

"Maybe so," Brice allowed. "That still doesn't provide proof that he's guilty of anything except wanting to build condos on every piece of land in the Hill Country that boasts a fine view."

A chorus of disgusted groans met that observation. "So far only some of the low-landers have sold out. Good ranch land, but not the vistas like this one that would inspire the moneybag lawyers and doctors from Austin and San Antonio to buy the property for their weekend getaway houses," Grant said.

"True," Brice said. "So why would he want that land? It's not like he can build some big housing development out in the middle of nowhere. The roads from Whiskey River aren't wide enough, and the speed limits are too low for people to want to live here and commute into San Antonio or Austin."

"I wouldn't put it past him to do it out of sheer meanness," Duncan said. "And the satisfaction of thinking he can get away with it."

"Maybe," Brice said. "But I'm thinking something about that land must be the key, if he is behind it. I thought I'd stop by the Whiskey River library later and look at the maps and property records. They have copies of some of the deed books from the county records office in Johnson City."

"Go for it, little brother," Grant said. "I should finish stringing the rest of the electric wire on the roadside boundary fences this week, so at least we'll know immediately if we have any more breaks. I've been thinking about installing some security cameras pointed at the gates too. Although someone bent on mischief could just cut the fences; they wouldn't need to open a gate."

"It might be worth it. Sometimes just having the bad guys know you've added surveillance is enough to convince them to attack someone else," Brice said.

Grant finished his bottled water. "Speaking of fencing, I'd better get back to work. Unlike you law enforcement wusses, who can lounge around waiting on court dates, we ranchers have to work every day."

"Why do you think he went into law enforcement?" Duncan said, grinning.

Brice gave him a narrow look. "Maybe I need to whup you instead of Grant. Yeah, we're wusses alright. Only have to get up before dawn and stay out all hours on a stakeout, track the bad guys through pouring rain or in the icy darkness, and get shot at by hostage-taking crazies."

Duncan and Grant sobered, exchanging looks. "We were sorry to hear about Tad. Seriously, we appreciate what you do, protecting us. And the dangers you face. Take care of yourself, won't you?"

"Always. Sorry to be touchy. It's only been a week since the funeral, though."

He'd lost one of his best friends from the police academy days ten days ago—shot in the face while doing a routine traffic stop for a burned-out taillight. But the driver had been a mule for a drug dealer, and panicking about being pulled over, had opened fire as soon as Tad tapped on his window.

The cost of the game. All the brothers knew that Brice, detailed out of the Texas Rangers Special Operations Division in Austin, and a sharpshooter when a SWAT squad was called out, could be the one in the sights of a gun-toting criminal someday.

"Well, thanks for meeting me for lunch," Brice said, trying to return to a more upbeat mood.

"Will you be around Whiskey River for a while?" Duncan asked.

"A few days, probably. Might as well stay here rather than go back to Austin. It's a shorter drive to the courthouse in Johnson City."

"You're welcome to bunk in at the house," Duncan offered.

"Or stay here at the cabin," Grant said.

"Hmm . . . take up residence with one of my newlywed brothers? Probably not. I might camp up at our old site on the ridge. Or I could get a room at Hell's Half Acre B&B downtown, where I could walk to the Diner or Booze's or the steakhouse if I'm wanting something fancy."

Grant grinned. "That might be fitting. The swinging single dude staying in a former bordello."

Duncan shook his head. "You might not want to stay with us, but you know our lovely wives are at least going to want to feed you if you stay in the area."

"Well, I might not turn down an invite to some meals."

"I should think not," Duncan said. "I do a better steak than Barron's, and Grant makes some mean tacos and enchiladas."

"Dinners for sure, then," Brice said. "I'll text you and let you know my plans."

The threesome rose and carried their drinks and takeout bags back into the cabin. "We'll look to see you again soon, then, little brother," Duncan said.

"Thanks for hosting us for lunch at the cabin," Brice said. "It's still the best view in three counties."

"Anytime," Grant said. "With you chasing the bad guys all over Central Texas, we don't get to see you all that often."

"Well, I'll try not to hang around long enough for you to tire of my company," Brice said.

"Good luck at the library," Duncan said. "I hope you turn up something useful."

AN HOUR LATER, after checking into a room at the B&B and parking his truck in the lot, Brice blew out a breath of relief as he walked into the cool air-conditioned dimness of the Whiskey River library. Even at midday, the high ridge on which Grant's cabin was located got a good breeze, and sitting in the shade on the deck, being outdoors had still been pleasant. After walking two blocks in town from the B&B, with no breeze and heat rising in waves off the roads and sidewalks, though, the air-conditioning felt great.

Not that he'd ever admit it to his brothers, he thought, smiling, unless he wanted to get ribbed about going soft. They'd all grown up cutting hay, chasing down stray cows, and mending fencing all through the year. Ranch work didn't stop for weather, whether the stifling heat of late summer or the cold driving rain of January. His boyhood spent in the open had prepared him well for August's two-a-day football practices in high school too.

But being able to tolerate the heat and enjoying it were two different things.

Though, being off duty, he wasn't wearing a badge, most of the patrons in the reading room still looked up as he walked over to the librarian's desk. A broad-shouldered former offensive lineman who stood six foot six, in jeans, boots, a western shirt and signature white Stetson, tended to attract attention even without the Ranger star on his chest.

Most of patrons here, though, were longtime residents he knew well. Respecting the library silence rules, they threw him a wave or a nod rather than calling out a greeting. Walking up to the desk, he doffed his hat and smiled at Shirley Lane, who'd been the head librarian as long as he could remember.

"Hi, Miss Shirley. How are you?" he said in a low voice.

"Why Brice McAllister, as I live and breathe! My, you're looking good—all grown up and a Texas Ranger!" She shook her head.

"Yeah, I expect you thought I would end up behind bars rather than holding the keys," he teased.

"Now you three boys kicked up some larks growing up, but I always knew you were good kids. How have you been?"

"Doing fine. And you?"

"Well, it's been a bit lonely since I lost Warren, but I'm managing. What brings you in?"

"I want to look at the old and current county maps. Then match them up to the deeds of ownership and maybe tax records of income tax paid on mineral rights. Where would I find those?"

"The maps are all kept in the reference room. Some of them are fragile, so I'm afraid you can't borrow them. But you're welcome to look at them and take any notes you want. The original deeds and tax records are at the county courthouse in Johnson City, but for a small fee, you can access them online."

"Great. Let me pay you the fee, and then I'll go look at the maps. In the reference room, you said?"

"Yes. Mary Williams is the reference librarian. Tell her what you need and she'll pull out the maps for you."

"Thank you, ma'am," he said, giving her a nod.

"You need anything else, just let me know."

After paying his fee and thanking Shirley for her help, he walked down a short hallway to the reference room, where rare, fragile, or historic books and records were kept. In addition to walls of bookshelves and cabinets with wide, shallow drawers that held the maps, the room contained tables and chairs where patrons could sit while they viewed the materials, several of them also holding desktop computers linked into the library internet system.

The room was empty except for a dark-haired woman who was facing away from him, replacing some books on a shelf. "Hello, ma'am," Brice called out when he walked in, not wanting to startle her. "Miss Shirley said you'd help me find some maps."

The woman turned toward him. "Certainly, sir. Which maps do you need?"

Her name hadn't rung a bell, and when she turned to face him, he confirmed that he had never met her. Tall for a woman, which made the top of her head reach about to his chin. Lustrous dark hair pulled back severely into a bun. Dark eyes that might be pretty, although the heavy dark-rimmed glasses she wore made it difficult to tell. Skin with a slight olive tint said she might be Hispanic, despite the bland Anglo name. Which might have been a married name, except Brice noted she wasn't wearing a wedding ring.

She was, however, wearing a dark, shapeless, long-sleeved dress made out of some sort of material that looked like burlap that might just be the ugliest thing he'd ever seen on a woman. Though by her unlined face and air of vitality, he'd estimate her to be about his own age—late twenties, maybe—the granny hairdo and unattractive clothing made her seem older.

Smiling, he held out his hand. "Brice McAllister, Miss Williams. I grew up around here—you may know my brothers, Duncan and Grant, who run our family place, the Triple A ranch. I don't recall seeing you around town before, so you must be new here."

She gave him a brief smile, but didn't shake his hand. "I've worked at the library for about a year. Now, what was it you wanted me to find for you, Mr. McAllister?"

He didn't consider himself irresistible to women, but Brice usually got a warmer response to an introduction and a smile than that.

O-kay, so she didn't do friendly. Must be from a big city somewhere. Taking the time to say hello and chat briefly when you encountered someone was pretty much the minimum standard of politeness in a small town like Whiskey River.

But he could do all business, too, if that was what she preferred.

"I'd like to look at all the city and county maps, from the first surveys to the last. Also, access deed records and property taxes, which Miss Shirley told me I could do online. I paid her the fee."

She nodded. "If you'll have a seat at one of the tables, I'll locate the maps and bring them over, along with the network password and the internet address for the county deeds and records office."

He did as instructed, choosing a table near the window where the light would be good. Once he had the map location and owners pinned down, he could check to see whether taxes had ever been paid for mineral rights on any of the properties. There were lucrative deposits of oil and gas all over Texas, the nearby Permian Basin containing one of the largest.

He could understand Marshall Thomason wanting to buy out ranchers who might be sitting on valuable oil reserves, but as far as he knew, there was no guarantee the Triple A had any. They had certainly never authorized any company to explore and find out. So why would Thomason want their land?

Maybe he didn't. Maybe, if he was in fact behind the incidents, it *was* just pure meanness, trying to aggravate a man his name and status didn't impress, who'd never shown him the deference Thomason felt his wealth and his important family connections deserved.

With nothing to do but wait, Brice found himself watching Miss No-Nonsense Librarian. With her severe hairdo, glasses and ugly dress, she could be a caricature of the Old Maid Librarian, despite the pretty eyes he noticed behind the heavy glasses. What had soured her on life?

Her demeanor might shout "old maid—men stay away"

but her movements were graceful, almost athletic. Brice wondered if she'd been a gymnast or a dancer. Certainly she balanced the wide, unwieldy maps she was extracting from the map case with ease. He caught himself before he invited a snub by asking if he could give her a hand.

Miss Williams would probably tell him, with a disapproving stare, that she was fully capable of Doing It All Herself.

The occupational hazard of law enforcement—meeting someone, he instinctively began to evaluate them, figure out their background, and decide whether the way they presented themselves matched their appearance. Miss Mary Williams was something of a puzzle. But he figured if the woman had had a bad experience with men and wanted to avoid them, becoming a reference librarian where she dealt mostly with dusty maps and moldy papers was probably an excellent occupation.

Dressing like she did, too, would eliminate any second looks that might notice the pretty eyes and dark hair and prompt a man to try to get to know her better.

A few minutes later, after extracting a card from her desk drawer and scrawling a note on it, she brought the maps over and spread them carefully on a table adjacent to the one he'd chosen with the computer.

"Some of the maps are too large to fit on the computer table, so I'll leave them here. You can review them and move over to do your online search. Here's the password and

URL." She handed him the card. "You may view the maps for as long as you like, or until the library closes. As I'm sure Miss Shirley told you, reference materials can't be checked out. Just leave them on the table when you are finished. I'll put them away later."

"Thank you, Miss Williams," he said, trying another smile.

Which received no more response than the first. Returning a short nod, Mary Williams walked back to her desk and back to her work, doing an excellent job of ignoring him.

FOR NEXT FEW hours, Brice looked over maps, checked the deed and tax records online and made some notes. Only a few of the farms and ranches on the back road along which Duncan told him Thomason had purchased properties had ever recorded paying taxes on mineral rights or royalties. Even on those, the amounts paid were low, indicating that the area probably wasn't rich with easily obtainable oil and gas. If the reserves on the ranches that had been tapped were modest, there was less likelihood that a neighboring property would contain a big enough bonanza of oil, gas, onyx or gypsum to make it worthwhile for Thomason to purchase it.

Of course, he'd only done a cursory search. Warranty deeds for property that didn't specifically mention the mineral rights supposedly indicated those rights belonged to the property owners. But sometimes, previous owners leased or sold mineral rights without filing a separate mineral rights deed, leaving the status of the mineral rights cloudy, even if the new owner had a valid warranty deed. New landowners in Texas were always advised to have a detailed title search done before they tried to exploit any mineral assets on their property, a laborious and often expensive proposition.

Given the little he'd uncovered, he didn't think it probable that Thomason, more concerned about his own profits than enriching anyone else, would have wanted to hire the expensive expertise of a "landman," a specialist whose sole job was to trace out mineral rights from surface property rights, usually on behalf of an oil or gas company interested in drilling on the property.

The only thing the properties possessed in common was a border along the county road that formed the western barrier of the Triple A. Which, his instincts told him, if Thomason were trying to sabotage operations and make the Triple A so unprofitable that Duncan and Grant were forced to sell off part of the land, it didn't appear to have anything to do with mineral rights.

Still, the fact that the property bordered the Triple A made him suspect that, if there were in fact harassment and Thomason was behind it, the reason still had to be something about the land. Though he had no idea what.

Standing, he stretched out his back, stiff from bending over the maps, and walked over to the reference desk, where

Miss Williams sat working on a desktop computer. "I'm finished with them, ma'am," he said. "Sure I can't bring them over to the desk for you?"

"No, thank you, I'd prefer to handle them myself."

Miss Shirley would have asked him if he'd found what he needed, or whether she could get him something else, or at least bid him goodbye. Mary Williams, after giving him another short nod he took as a dismissal, returned her attention to her computer and went back to ignoring him.

It shouldn't have annoyed him—what did it matter whether Whiskey River's reference librarian liked him or not? But her barely polite demeanor and extreme disinterest seemed . . . deliberate, somehow. Not antagonistic, exactly, but . . . wary.

Why should a woman he'd never met before be wary of him?

The question tweaking his lawman's curiosity even further, with a frown, he walked out.

Chapter Two

MARY KEPT HER eyes on her computer until the sound of Brice McAllister's footsteps faded, then breathed out a sigh of relief. She'd known who he was as soon as he said his name, though he hadn't known her. She'd made it her business to find out everything she could about the local families when she moved to Whiskey River, wanting to evaluate who she might safely see, and who she should avoid—like anyone connected with law enforcement. Not that she personally had any reason to avoid officers of the law, but better to know who she might be dealing with, so she could prevent any unpleasant surprises.

The last person she wanted to get to know better was a Texas Ranger. Simply being aware of what he did for a living had made her nervous and edgy the whole time he was in the room. Though part of that unease, she acknowledged, was due to the fact that despite her wariness, disturbingly, she still found him attractive.

Tall, broad-shouldered, powerfully built, he looked like the football player she's heard he'd been. In addition to that attractive frame and his handsome face, he'd employed a smile that could charm the panties off a nun to try to beguile her into opening up with him. Resisting that temptation had made her short to the point of rudeness, she thought ruefully, a little ashamed now at her curtness.

At least it meant she wouldn't have to worry about the alarming fact that she actually found him attractive. If her unflattering garb hadn't already discouraged him from wanting to further the acquaintance, her chilly demeanor certainly would.

She still wasn't interested in becoming friendly with any man, her response to even the handsomest usually a dull apathy. But she had to admit, for the first time since Ian's death, she'd felt . . . something. A niggle of attraction. A tiny crumb of interest.

For a *Texas Ranger*. How stupid was that? Proof positive that her brain still wasn't working normally about the subject of men.

He'd viewed his maps, taken some notes, and left without indicating he needed more time, so she didn't think he'd be returning. She knew he was based in Austin, so she was unlikely to see him around town very often.

Which, given her odd reaction to him, was a very good thing.

Which also meant she didn't need to waste any more time worrying about him or that atypical reaction. It was almost closing time. She'd refile the maps and head home.

HALF AN HOUR later, the reference room tidied for the night, Mary walked out into the main library to see Shirley standing at her desk, keys in hand. "I was just going to come and see if you were ready to leave."

"On my way out," Mary confirmed.

"Good, I'll lock up behind you." As Mary reached the desk, Shirley added, "Well, what did you think?"

Mary looked at her blankly. She didn't recall her supervisor tasking her with something. "Think about what?"

Shirley shook her head in exasperation. "Honestly, dear, I begin to despair of you. About Brice McAllister, of course! He and his brothers are about the handsomest things in cowboy boots and Stetsons in Whiskey River, and he's the only single brother left. I've known all three since they were boys, and you couldn't find nicer, more courteous and considerate men anywhere. Their dear mother would have been proud. She died when they were young, you see. Their daddy brought in one of her cousins to help him with the boys. Ended up marrying her. Which he should have, because she's a wonderful lady and raised those boys right. Duncan, the oldest, runs the ranch, and Grant, after some time in the Marines, came back to help him. Brice went into law enforcement. Applied to become a Ranger once he had enough time in and got the appointment—which is quite a feat. They don't take many. He doesn't get to town too often, but you might look for him when he does. Couldn't find a finer young man and I guarantee, he knows how to treat a lady."

Mary listened patiently. Shirley was a kind boss and a sweet woman who'd gone above and beyond to look out for Mary when she first arrived in Whiskey River, recommending a cottage to rent and helping her settle in. But as an older widow from a previous generation, she was certain Mary's life couldn't be satisfying or complete without a man in it. She made a point of discussing any single man who came to the reference room who showed even remotest potential of becoming husband material.

Mary had to admit, Brice McAllister was the most attractive of all the men Shirley had urged on her. She felt a momentary pang of—regret, perhaps, or sadness—at what her solitary life might be causing her to miss.

Maybe someday, she'd feel ready to explore the possibility of including a man in her life again. Someday, a long time from now.

"If he's that handsome, charming, and well brought up, I'm sure he doesn't lack for feminine company."

"A good man needs a good woman; that's all I'm saying," Shirley said. "Couldn't do better, if he interested you, and you'd be good for him too. A nice, intelligent, hardworking girl like you who behaves like a real lady is hard to find these days. Most young women are so flighty, flirting with anything in pants. And the way they dress! Strutting down the street in clothes so tight and revealing, it's as if walking there were their profession."

"Not a fan of skintight jeans and halter tops?"

Shirley shuddered. "Certainly not on women of my age. You'd think they would know better. Even the younger ones need to be slim and shapely for it to be attractive, though it's still too revealing, in my opinion. I much prefer your modest dresses."

Mary suppressed a smile. Apparently the older woman had jumped off the style train so long ago, she didn't see the difference between "modest" and "downright unflattering."

"Thanks, Shirley. I do appreciate you looking out for me."

Shirley sighed. "I just wish I could do more. It's one thing for me, who had thirty wonderful years with my Warren, to go home to an empty house. I just hate to see you, with all you have to offer, spending your life all alone."

"You don't need to worry," Mary reassured her with a smile. "I'm never alone. I have wonderful neighbors. And my books."

"Maybe so, but I'd rather you had something a little warmer to cuddle up with at night than the latest novel! But I've nagged you enough. Have a good evening, dear. I'll see you tomorrow."

"Yes, see you then. Good night," Mary said, walking out so the head librarian could lock up after her.

It might be nice to have something warm to cuddle up

with at night, Mary thought as she walked to her car.

Maybe she should get a dog.

SHE MIGHT BE the only occupant of her house, but it still made her smile every time she pulled into her driveway. The little craftsman cottage with its pretty front porch, wide old pine floors, large windows, living room with fireplace, tidy kitchen with a tiny dining nook and deck overlooking a large backyard, was everything she'd wanted when she moved from the big city to the sleepy town of Whiskey River.

After all the pain and loss, despite the loneliness, it warmed her heart to walk into a place that was exactly what she'd always imagined she, Ian and their children would live in.

"You would have loved it, Ian," she said aloud before she caught herself. Would she ever stop talking to him? Although it had been more than three years now since she'd lost him, he still occupied such a large part of her heart she sometimes had trouble believing he was really gone.

Nor was there anyone to overhear her. Living far away from everything and everyone she'd once loved, if it comforted her to talk to him, what did it matter?

She did talk with real people, too, after all. Shirley at work, and her next-door neighbors. She smiled again as she pictured Bunny's crooked smile. The little girl was insatiably curious about everything and seemed to enjoy spending time with Mary as much as Mary enjoyed her company. Her mom, Elaine, had become a good friend and Bunny's dad, Tom, a mortgage banker in town, was going to help Mary arrange to buy the cottage, now that she'd decided she would settle in Whiskey River permanently.

She hadn't been sure exactly what she was looking for when she'd moved half a continent away from the place she grew up, except that she was certain that life as she'd always known it was no longer possible. She'd sought the complete opposite: a small town with a sleepy pace, isolation from family, reliance only on herself.

Whiskey River had given her a fresh start and more. A job she enjoyed—what reading fanatic wouldn't love being surrounded all day by books? A boss who encouraged and supported her. A lovely home she'd been able to furnish exactly to her taste. A backyard large enough to plant the garden of her dreams, though she was still learning which plants would survive in the brutal Texas summers. Neighbors who were kind and supportive without being nosy and intrusive. And Bunny, the sweet child she would never have, whose kind parents allowed her to borrow as often as she liked.

Maybe she'd harvest some tomatoes and fresh basil before she made dinner and cook up some tomato sauce to bring over when she babysat Bunny this weekend. Or better still, she'd wait until Bunny came over and have the six-year-old help her. The child loved poking around her extensive garden and seemed to always find it amazing that they could turn into dinner something she picked herself.

Maybe she'd show Bunny how to make homemade pasta to go with the tomato sauce.

A bittersweet warmth welled up. She might never stop mourning that she couldn't have a child of her own, but Bunny's presence in her life was a precious, special blessing.

With a fulfilling job, a cozy cottage, good friends who lived next door, and a charmer like Bunny to love, what did Mary need with a man?

ON A SPARKLING sunny morning two days later, Brice walked the few blocks from the B&B to the home of his high school football buddy, Tom Edgerton. It had been several months since he'd had time to visit with Tom, his wife, Elaine, and their little girl, the six-year-old charmer who did him the honor of calling him "Uncle Brice."

He smiled as he approached the old rambling Victorian house with its large wraparound porch. Though it was much grander than the simple country ranch house Brice had grown up in, the Victorian, with its whimsical turrets and fishtail-siding details and that welcoming porch, had always seemed like a home ready to embrace family and friends.

After striding up the stairs, he rang the front doorbell. A

moment later, Elaine opened it. "Brice, welcome! I'm so glad you made the time to see us," she cried, giving him a hug. "Tom's out playing an early round of golf with the branch manager, but he should be back soon."

"The branch manager? I take it this golf game is more work than pleasure."

"True, although he does like the guy, fortunately. Coffee's in the carafe and the blueberry scones are about ready."

"Sounds great! You're looking well! How go the yoga classes?"

"I've had a great enrollment this summer. In addition to my usual adult classes, I started one for high school girls. Yoga is so good for balance, poise, and toning the body. Just the thing to bolster the self-esteem of high schoolers, who so often need the boost."

"Speaking of girls, where's my sweetheart?"

"Bunny's overnighting with a school friend, but she'll be home by noon. When she found out you were coming this morning, she almost made me call her mother's friend and cancel the overnight! She wouldn't miss a chance to see Uncle Brice."

"I can't wait to see her."

As she walked him into the kitchen, she said, "Pour yourself a coffee. The scones are already in the oven, so they won't take long. It's such a pretty morning—not beastly hot yet—I thought we'd sit and eat them out on the back porch."

"Great idea. Although your scones are delicious no matter when I eat them."

She laughed. "Save a few for Tom, please. Why don't you take your coffee and go on out? I'll join you with the scones when they're ready."

After pouring a mugful, Brice walked out onto the large, shaded porch that overlooked an expanse of neatly trimmed lawn, with a play set for Bunny on one side and a flagstone terrace in the center, bordered by beds of rosemary, lantana, and Lady in Red salvia, now a riot of red, gold, and orange blooms.

Settling into a chair, Brice took a long swig of coffee and sighed with pleasure. Was there anything finer than sitting on a back porch sipping coffee, while a soft breeze wafted over the sharp scent of herbs and the early sun set the whole landscape glittering?

He was staring into the distance, enjoying the moment, when a flash of motion in the neighboring backyard caught his eye. Focused on the movement, he saw someone facing away from him, bent over at the waist, weeding what looked like a bed of cherry tomatoes.

A female someone, with long, shapely bare legs and tight short shorts that barely covered a cute little behind impossible to ignore, since the lady's torso and head were bent to the ground and shadowed by it.

Smiling, Brice waited with anticipation for the woman to stand up. The view when she did was just as pleasing. That tempting butt narrowed to a slim waist and a halter top that displayed a lovely swath of lightly tanned back. Long, curly black hair tossed up casually in a high ponytail completed the appealing picture.

It took him a moment to realize Elaine had walked out and spoken to him.

"Who is that?" he asked, turning toward her.

She laughed. "My neighbor. Who, I agree, is well worth looking at. She's fairly new to Whiskey River, so you might not have met her."

"I assure you I have not. Why don't you correct that dreadful mistake?"

Elaine wagged a warning finger at him. "Okay, I'll introduce you, but hold back on the charm. You're a player, but she's not, so don't be thinking of some overnight quickie affair."

Brice put a hand over his heart. "You wound me! You know I don't use 'em, abuse 'em and cast 'em aside."

"True. But . . . it's complicated. You see—"

"Better call her quick," Brice interrupted. "Looks like she's heading inside."

Elaine gave him a measuring look.

Brice held up his hands. "I'll be on my best behavior. Promise."

"You'd better be," Elaine muttered. Going to stand at the porch railing, she waved and called out, "Hey, neighbor! Can you come over for some coffee?"

The woman turned and waved back, putting up a hand to block the sun shining directly into her eyes. "Morning, Elaine. Sure, I have a minute."

The view from a distance had been attractive and it was even better as she walked closer. From the ebony curls to the pert nose with a hint of freckles and the lush, kissable mouth, his gaze drifted down to admire the halter top's display of full breasts with a hint of cleavage, more golden tanned skin on her bare arms and midriff, then rose back up to appreciate her beautiful dark eyes.

Those eyes. For an instant, he had the impression he'd met her before, but he couldn't place where.

"I want to introduce a good friend," Elaine said as the lady drew closer. "Mary, this is Tom's best high school buddy, Brice McAllister. Brice, my best neighbor, Mary Williams."

The woman stopped short. "We've already met," she said, her smile disappearing. "You'll have to excuse me. I don't think I have time for that coffee after all."

She turned on her heel and walked back to her cottage.

Elaine looked at him, her jaw dropped in surprise. "Good grief, Brice! What did you do to offend her?"

He had a hard time understanding her words, his startled brain scrambling to reconcile two shockingly different images. That hot babe in short shorts and halter top . . . was the same woman as the dowdy librarian? Shaking his head to try to make sense of it, he said, "Mary Williams. The reference librarian in town?"

Elaine nodded. "What did you do? Destroy a first edition?"

"I didn't do anything!" he protested. "I met her a few days ago when I went to consult some old maps in the reference room. But . . . she didn't look anything like that!"

Elaine laughed. "I know. I've tried to tactfully talk to her about the way she dresses for work, but she politely evades me. Aside from her terrible taste in clothes, she's a wonderful person. Bunny absolutely adores her. I have to rein her in, or she'd be over there every minute Mary is home. She's so warm and patient and loving with her. Reads her stories, shows her how to garden, cooks with her, plays games. Even got Bunny her own child-size garden tools and gloves. She's a terrific cook too. Always whipping up some amazing Italian dish and bringing some of it over, saying she's made too much and doesn't want to eat it for a week. Tom leaps at the chance, I'll tell you. It's been great having her there. She's offered to babysit whenever we need her. It's so nice to know we have someone dependable so close by, so we can go out and really enjoy ourselves, knowing Bunny is having just as much fun as we are."

Brice was still having trouble putting together the dowdy librarian and the hot babe. "She doesn't seem very friendly."

"Well . . . now that you mention it, she's not very friendly to men. She must be really resistant if she didn't respond to you, since you can usually charm the fleas off a dog. As far as I've seen, she never goes out with anyone, not even girlfriends. Aside from us and Miss Shirley, I don't think she's made any friends in Whiskey River. I've suggested she go down to happy hour at Booze's or to Buddy's Bar & Boogie, the new honky-tonk out on the highway. Someplace where she could meet other young single people her age, but she said she's not much for the bar scene."

Elaine fell silent, looking troubled.

"What?" Brice asked, instantly picking up on her unease.

"It's just that I . . . worry about her sometimes. She never has any visitors. She never talks about family, or about anything, really, that happened to her before she came to Whiskey River. When I think back, it took even us a really long time to get to know her. Kept to herself. It was Bunny who broke the ice—you know she never met a stranger. A year ago in the spring, must have been six months or so after Mary moved in, a nice sunny Saturday morning, Bunny saw her in the yard, planting a garden, and just had to go over and find out what she was doing."

Brice smiled. "Sounds like Bunny."

"Mary was super nice to her, explained what she was planting, even let Bunny help a little. But she only gradually warmed up to us, brushing off our invitations to dinner or lunch or coffee for the longest time. She doesn't seem wary of Tom, but the way she avoids people, especially men, makes me suspect she might have run from a bad situation."

"Domestic abuse, you mean?"

Elaine nodded. "Yeah. I think she might have an abusive ex-boyfriend or ex-husband that makes her want to avoid getting into another romantic relationship. It's not relationships in general, because since getting to know her, she's been a good neighbor and she's great with Bunny. It's just . . . men."

"Even charming men?"

Elaine gave him a look. "Don't take it in your head that she's a challenge and you need to charm or coax or persuade her into going out with you. I won't have you harassing her."

Irritated, Brice retorted, "Now I'm really insulted. You know I wasn't brought up like that. Miss Dorothy would have whupped me from here to Sunday if I ever bothered or harassed a lady."

"Good. I thought so, but Mary is awfully pretty, so I can see that trying to get her to like you might be tempting. If you do anything about her, you might keep an eye out. If she is on the run from an abusive ex, it would be good to have a Texas Ranger in her court if he managed to find her. Don't push her too hard trying to get to know her, but I would feel better if you kept tabs—discreetly—on any potential situation."

Brice frowned. "Nothing I despise more than a man who mistreats women. If that is the case, I'd want to take his head off. You and Tom keep an eye out too. Let me know if you notice anyone hanging around or looking suspicious."

"Oh, we do watch out—suspecting what we suspect.

She's such a sweetheart, it makes me sick to think that someone might have hurt her. I hope she can eventually get beyond whatever happened, because as great as she is with kids and with her being such a terrific cook, she'd make someone a wonderful wife."

Brice held up hands in a warding-off gesture. "Not in the market."

Elaine grinned. "I thought that might discourage you. Mary is definitely the homey-wife type, not hot-sex-babe material."

"Elaine, please!" he protested, laughing. "You'll make me blush."

She gave a snort of disbelief. "Right. I'll believe that."

"Honey, where are you?" A voice called from inside the house.

"On the back porch, Tom," Elaine called back. "Pour yourself some coffee and come on out."

Her husband, Tom, big, broad-shouldered, and tall like Brice, had been a fellow offensive lineman in high school who'd gone on to play college ball at the University of Texas before turning his business degree into a lucrative job in mortgage banking back home. He came out onto the porch carrying his coffee, then leaned over to give his wife a kiss. "Blueberry scones, whoa-daddy!" he said, spying the plate in the center of the table. "You know the road to a man's heart."

"There are still some left, amazingly, despite Brice getting here before you. He was too mesmerized, watching Mary garden in her short shorts, to remember to eat."

"If I weren't married to the most beautiful woman in Texas, I might understand what you mean," Tom said with a grin.

Elaine batted her husband on the nose. "Look all you like, as long as you bring me home from the dance."

"Darlin', you know there's only you. Brice, sure was good to get your text and know you were in the area. But what brings you to downtown Whiskey River?"

"I'm waiting to testify at a court case in Johnson City, which probably will happen on Monday, then I'll head back to Austin. Thought I'd take advantage of the break and stay downtown."

"At the B&B? You and your brothers have a falling out?"

"Tom, neither of them has been married six months yet."

"Oh, yeah, there's that. Well, you could have stayed with us."

"I didn't want to impose."

Tom gave him a look. "I sure hope you know us well enough to know it's never an imposition to have a friend we count as close as family come stay with us. Though you might have been wise not to. Bunny would be sure to dog your every step."

"Unless Mary invited her to come over and cook or garden," Elaine said. "You have a rival for your affection now, Brice."

“She does love Mary,” Tom said. “Can’t blame her. What’s not to love when you have someone who’ll do whatever you want to do, cooks you whatever you like, and is ready to read stories and play games all night? Mary focuses on what Bunny wants more than her own grandma does—and she looks a lot better.”

“Bunny spends a lot of time there, then?” Brice asked.

“She’d practically live there if we didn’t intervene,” Tom said, confirming what Elaine had told him earlier. “Good thing she’s such a nice lady.”

Was she a nice lady? Brice’s lawman instincts went on high alert anytime he was presented with two images of someone that were as different as “Homely Librarian” and “Hot Gardener.”

But Tom and Elaine were no fools, and they were very protective of their daughter. If they both thought Mary Williams was a safe person for Bunny to know, she probably was. Probably.

“The fruit is cut and it will take just a minute to fix the omelets,” Elaine said. “Shall we go in and eat in the kitchen? It’s already getting pretty warm out here.”

Tom stood up. “Yes, let’s. Maybe after, we could turn on the game. Houston’s playing a doubleheader.”

“Sounds great,” Brice said.

But he remained troubled. A woman with no friends, no visitors, who never went out or mentioned family. What if she were running from something other than an abusive situation?

Bad guys were not always guys; sometimes they were girls. When he met her at the library, he hadn't gotten a warning vibe that hinted she might be involved in some sort of criminal activity, but something had definitely been off. She'd been very curt and visibly nervous.

He didn't want to alarm Elaine or Tom, when his innate caution might be completely unwarranted. But since the woman was spending a lot of time alone with Bunny, *his* Bunny, he wanted to be sure there was nothing in her past that might make her a danger to the little girl.

Tucking his observations in the back of his mind, Brice followed them in for brunch. He'd do some quiet investigating on his own, just to make sure Bunny was safe.

Chapter Three

THE MIDDLE OF the following week, Brice drove from Johnson City back to Tom and Elaine's in Whiskey River. His testimony at the trial was concluded, and since he hadn't gotten to spend much time with Bunny on his previous visit, he'd promised her to come and overnight with the Edgertons before heading home.

He'd taken advantage of some free time during trial recesses to nip back to his office in Austin and do some background checking. His conscience tweaked him a little to be investigating a citizen not under suspicion of any crime, but he assured himself that protecting the wellbeing of a child justified a little snooping. Since Texas law required new residents moving in from out of state to get a Texas driver's license within a year, and he'd seen the librarian's car parked in the driveway by her cottage, it had been easy enough to pull up her driver's license, although he had to wade through fifty or so other "Mary Williams" before he found the correct one. Then he'd used that picture—which, fortunately, showed her with hair down rather than pulled back into a severe bun—to run a facial recognition check through state and federal data banks.

He'd been reassured when the system returned only "low probability" matches and needed only a cursory further inspection to confirm that none of the images resembled Mary Williams.

So his initial instincts were correct; if she was running from something, it wasn't because she'd been incarcerated or was wanted for any crime.

Next, he ran a quick license check in several other states to see if he could find where she'd lived before coming to Whiskey River. And came up with no matches—at least, not for the Mary Williams who worked at the library and lived next door to Bunny. "Williams" being a pretty common surname, there were literally hundreds of "Mary Williams" with driver's licenses. If she'd married and divorced, she might have gotten a new license with her maiden name, but if "Williams" were her maiden name, with most young people getting driver's licenses at sixteen, he would have expected to find a record of a license for a younger Mary Williams.

He found *nada* that matched her picture.

But there are a lot of states. It would take forever to check through them all.

By the end of his investigations, he'd begun to suspect that "Mary Williams" was not in fact her original name. If she did want to evade discovery, changing her name to something for which anyone searching would encounter hundreds or thousands of matches would be good tactic.

If she had legally changed her name, he'd need to know the county in which the name change had been registered to be able to trace her former name in court records. And if she had been in a domestic abuse situation, the name change could have been made confidential, with no public notice given and the records sealed, so that anyone searching under her former name would not be able to discover what her new name was.

He ended up guiltily relieved that his snooping hadn't turned up anything that showed she might pose a danger to Bunny. But he also tended to share Elaine's fear that "Mary Williams" might be hiding from someone.

It would be hard to keep an eye on her and ensure her safety unless he could somehow make her less wary of him. For that, he thought with a smile as he turned onto the Edgertons' street, he was counting on Bunny.

HIS SCHEME WORKED just as beautifully as he'd hoped. After sending Elaine and Tom off for a matinee movie to be followed by a romantic dinner, he took Bunny out on the back porch for lemonade and to play a favorite game of *go fish*. And as he'd hoped, a little after the library's closing time, he heard a car pull into the driveway next door.

Half an hour later, Mary Williams came out her back

door and headed to her garden. Not in short shorts and a halter top this time, sadly, but the sleeveless cotton dress in a floral pattern looked cool and summery and was a thousand times more attractive than the dress she'd worn the day he'd first met her at the library.

Bunny spotted her immediately. "Hey, Miss Mary!" she cried, running down the steps and over to the fence. "Can I help you pick vegetables?"

The beautiful smile she gave the child sent a jolt of surprise—and intense attraction—through Brice. It transformed her face, already pretty without the dark glasses, making her luminous eyes sparkle, turning those tempting lips into a bow, and giving her an air of engaging warmth that had been totally missing in the woman on the previous two occasions he'd seen her.

Hoo-wee! As the recipient of a smile like that, no wonder Bunny had been drawn to her.

"Sure, Bunny, if it's okay with your mommy. I don't want to make you late for dinner."

"Mommy's not cooking dinner. She and Daddy are on a date!" The girl smiled mischievously. "That means they'll come home all kissy and huggy and send me to bed early."

Mary laughed. "It's good for your mommy and daddy to be kissy and huggy. But if they are out, who's watching you?"

"Uncle Brice. If I pick some vegetables, can I help you make something for dinner? You're a much better cook than he is."

Brice knew the exact minute Mary's gaze swung from Bunny to the porch. Meeting her startled eyes, he descended the back steps and walked to the fence to join Bunny. Slow, casual, nonthreatening.

"Hi, Miss Williams. I'd like to say my cooking skills have just been unfairly maligned, but that would be lying. I can do breakfast, sandwiches, burgers and steaks on the grill—bachelor survival fare—but nothing fancy."

"See?" Bunny said. "We *need* to cook with you! Please?"

"I ought to be wounded that I came back to town just to spend an evening with my best girl and she's ready to abandon me for her new friend."

"I won't abandon you," Bunny said indignantly. "You can cook too. Can't he, Miss Mary?"

Mary's eyes had widened and distress over the dilemma Bunny had created was written on her face. Clearly, she didn't want to disappoint Bunny, but she was also not at all happy at the idea of inviting a stranger into her home.

"I can go back to Elaine and Tom's, if you want, and let Bunny eat with you," he said quietly. "I don't want to make you uncomfortable."

"Don't go away, Uncle Brice! He can stay, can't he, Mary? He isn't a good cook, but he's lots of fun. He's really good at games and he always makes me laugh. He can make you laugh too."

Not answering him, and with an uneasy smile, she focused on Bunny. "What do you want to make? There's not enough time to simmer a tomato sauce from scratch, but we could make the chicken dish you like. The one where you get to pound the chicken with the meat mallet."

"Yes, that one! It's so much fun!"

"Let's have a salad too. Why don't you get a basket from the porch and pick some tomatoes, green peppers and a cucumber? Twist off the tomatoes, and use the special snips I got you to cut the stems of the peppers and cucumbers, like I showed you. Wear your gloves, too, because the cucumber spines can be sharp."

As the girl rushed off, Mary turned to Brice. "Please stay. We . . . kinda got off on the wrong foot. I probably owe you an apology. I'm . . . really shy and not very good with strangers. Meeting someone new is hard. As I'm sure you noticed, I just want to retreat. But you did nothing to offend me, and I'm sorry I was so, well, rude."

Relieved that his approach wasn't going to fail after all, her apology raised his spirits and confirmed his instincts. If Mary Williams were running from something, it wasn't after doing something nefarious.

"Apology accepted. Are you sure you want to invite me? I won't be offended if you'd rather just have Bunny—because I can see the chances of getting her to come back to her house before she gets you to make her dinner are about zero. I am a stranger, after all."

For a moment, he was afraid she'd accept the exit he'd

offered. But then, thankfully, she shook her head. "No, please stay. Bunny would be terribly disappointed if you didn't join us. You are a stranger, but Tom and Elaine, as well as Bunny, have given you a sterling recommendation."

"That's reassuring. If you're certain . . ."

When she nodded to confirm it, he smiled. "Thanks, then, I'd love to stay. I'll see if I can validate Bunny's confidence in me and make you laugh."

She smiled back at that. "Good luck."

Not sure whether that was a challenge or taunt, he followed her across the yard to the back porch, where she picked up another basket and went to help Bunny harvest the vegetables. A few snips of vines later, the three of them walked into the cottage.

After entering, Brice stopped and looked around admiringly. The cottage was small, but the beadboard wainscoting and walls painted a light tan, airy gauze curtains, accent pieces in blues, teals and tan, and a few well-chosen, comfortable-looking furniture pieces made it look homey and inviting. To the right was the living room area, with a washed-denim overstuffed couch and chair arranged around an old trunk that served as a coffee table; on the left side sat a farmhouse-style dining table and several chairs; and straight ahead, an island with bar seating separated both areas from a neat, functional kitchen. The hallway he could glimpse to the far right probably led to bedrooms and a bathroom or two. And, as one might expect for a librarian's house, three of the walls in the great room held wall-to-ceiling bookshelves full of books and small decorative items.

"What a nice home you've made this into," Brice said. "I've only ever seen the cottage from the outside and always thought it looked inviting, but the interior is even more so. Warm, casual, homey. It feels like a man—or a child," he added, nodding toward Bunny, who was carrying the garden bounty into the kitchen, "could relax and enjoy themselves without stumbling over anything or breaking something."

"Thank you. I've always dreamed of living in a cottage, so furnishing it has been a pleasure. Home should be a comfortable place to live, not a fancy photo shoot for a design magazine."

"You've done a very good job of making it comfortable. My brother's wife, Abby, is an interior designer. She makes amazing furniture and fixtures out of yard sale finds, castoffs, and old kitchen equipment. This"—he gestured around the room—"reminds me of her style, a little more upscale. Have you been to her shop, Hidden Treasures? It's in the country not far outside Whiskey River. If you haven't, I think you'd enjoy visiting it."

"No, I haven't been there. I'll have to stop by. I collect old kitchen things—tea towels, utensils, cookware. I'd be interested to see what she makes from them. Can I get you some soda? Turn on the TV if you like, while Bunny and I start dinner."

"Just water, please. If it's okay, I'll sit at the island and help out, or watch, if I won't be in the way. At the least, I can cut up a salad."

"If you'd prefer."

He smiled and was delighted this time to get a tentative smile in return as he followed her over and took a seat at the island.

WHAT HAD SHE gotten herself into? Mary went to join Bunny at the kitchen sink, acutely aware of Brice McAllister seated at the island behind them. The cottage was small, he was a big man, and he seemed to suck up most of the air in the room, leaving her feeling—pressed.

But she hadn't seen any feasible way to avoid issuing the invitation. He was right—Bunny wouldn't want to go home without cooking dinner, and she would be disappointed if Brice didn't share it with them.

Taking a deep breath, Mary tried to tell herself to relax—despite the attraction that danced along her nerves again, annoyingly stronger than ever.

Stronger probably because the paean of praise Elaine had heaped on him had made her less wary of him, except for that unfortunate lawman status.

After Elaine apologized for springing him on her unannounced the other day, she'd gone on to enthuse about what a great friend he'd been to Tom, how he was a football jock in high school and college, the one all the girls make a play for, but he never let the attention go to his head. He always said, Elaine told her, that nothing can make a man humbler than growing up on a ranch, where the cows aren't impressed by you and nature is indifferent to your welfare, with every good year inevitably followed by one in which the operation hangs on by a shoestring. He'd dated a variety of women, but Elaine had never met an ex-girlfriend who had anything but regrets that such a nice guy wasn't interested in getting serious. He was also great with kids, which Mary had seen for herself in his interactions with Bunny.

He'd gone into law enforcement to protect people, Elaine told her. Maybe, she speculated, because he'd lost his mother when he was so young. He hadn't been able to save his mama, so now he was channeling that need into guarding the public at large.

"I'd never urge you to go out with someone," Elaine had concluded.

"Good. Because Shirley takes care of that," Mary had replied.

"But if you did decide to go out with someone, you couldn't find a nicer guy. He's not hard on the eyes, either."

Mary had to agree with that. He wasn't hard on the eyes, and the proximity of that big, powerful body sitting at her kitchen island created little tremors in the pit of her stomach. She could easily believe any woman under his care would feel protected.

Interestingly, though the size and sheer masculine energy he radiated made her keenly aware of him, she didn't feel menaced. Instead, she sensed that protective streak in the way he handled Bunny—not wanting to disappoint a child—and in his courtesy at allowing her the opportunity to exclude him, if having him in her home made her uncomfortable.

The feeling of being guarded was novel, a little unsettling, and far too appealing. She just needed to remember it was her own job to protect herself. And she would never be under his care.

The best way to avoid the unsettling effect he seemed to have on her would be to concentrate on Bunny and her cooking.

Suiting action to the thought, after handing Brice a cold water from the fridge, she turned to Bunny, who had carefully unloaded the two baskets of produce into the sink. "Wash your hands well, then rinse the tomatoes, cuke and peppers and leave them in the drainer. I have some fresh beans I harvested yesterday; you can get them from the crisper in the fridge. We'll roast them with salt and olive oil. I'll cut up some potatoes and we'll roast those, too, with rosemary."

Turning back to Brice, she said, "I'll get you a cutting board and a knife, if you really do want to cut up the salad. It's not necessary, I can—"

"No, I'd like to. Miss Dorothy, the cousin my dad asked

to come help us after Mom died, made sure all of us boys knew our way around the kitchen and were prepared to help out. Duncan and Grant turned out to be pretty good cooks. My skills are more rudimentary, maybe because I was the youngest, but I do know how to make salad."

"I'll let you demonstrate your skill." She brought him the cutting board and knife, then pulled out roasting pans for the green beans and potatoes and scooted a tall stool up to the island for Bunny, who had put the drained veggies into a salad bowl and carried it carefully over to the counter.

"Here you go, Uncle Brice," she said, handing it over. "Can I pound the chicken now, Miss Mary?"

"In a minute, *mimmo.* Get out the cling wrap while I take the chicken from the fridge."

Consciousness of Brice's gaze fixed on her made a prickly sensation skitter over her skin that she was trying hard to ignore. How odd, after she'd been more or less indifferent to men for years now, somehow he'd switched her dormant senses fully to "on."

They might be activated, but they weren't going to be indulged.

She got out the chicken and a bag of washed salad greens and brought them over to the island. "Put the greens in first, then cut up the tomatoes, cukes and green pepper."

"Any special way?"

"Halve, quarter or eighth the tomatoes, depending on size, halve the cucumber slices and cut the peppers into thin strips. Those are the things Bunny likes in a salad, but I also have onion, olives, cheese and marinated Italian peppers you can add to yours if you like."

"I do like—all those things."

"I'll get them out when we're ready to eat. Vegetables over to you," she said with a sweeping gesture. "Okay, *mimmo*, up you go," she said, helping Bunny climb up onto her seat.

Mary took the boneless chicken pieces, wrapped them in cling wrap, put them on the cutting board and let Bunny go after them with the mallet, which she did enthusiastically. Mary supervised while she cut up potatoes, mixed them and the already-cut green beans with sea salt and oil, and put them in their roasting pans. To her relief, Bunny chattered away, relieving her of the necessity of making conversation.

"Uncle Brice grew up on a ranch," Bunny was saying. "His brother Mr. Duncan lives there now. He has cows and horses. It's real pretty there! There are big hills and from the top you can see so far! And there's a little river at the bottom of the hill. Sometimes Uncle Brice takes me fishing."

"Uncle Brice doesn't live there now?" Mary asked. Encouraging Bunny to continue chatting—never a hard thing to manage—about her "Uncle Brice" would avoid any awkward silences and forestall McAllister from plying *her* with questions.

"No, he lives in the city. He's a Texas Ranger! He has a pretty star badge and a pistol and a rifle, but he doesn't bring those when he comes to visit us. Guns are dangerous and have to be kept locked up."

A shudder went through her as the memories she normally suppressed came flooding back. The report of a handgun at close range. Numb disbelief as blood blossomed under her fingers, followed by searing pain . . . . Wrenching her thoughts free, she said, "Absolutely. Guns are very dangerous."

"Sometimes Uncle Brice needs his gun, though, because there can be bad men who try to hurt people. He stops them." Bunny looked over at Brice with awe. "My daddy says he's very good at protecting people."

"That's the reason for the job, peanut," Brice said.

"Was that why you went into law enforcement?" Mary asked, still a little shaken and wondering if he'd confirm what Elaine had told her.

"Yes. I was always big for my age, so bullies never tried to pick on me. It would make me mad when they tried to take advantage of the smaller guys or tease the girls to tears. Growing up with two older brothers, I was pretty good with my fists, so I'd sort them out. Got me into trouble at school until I learned to be just as effective at talking them down as taking them down. Then, when I went out for football, the coaches encouraged me to play defensive line, since I was fast for my size. But I preferred offensive line, where I could protect the quarterback and running backs so they could make plays." He shrugged. "We boys always knew Duncan would take over the ranch when he grew up, so going into law enforcement as a career just seemed like the logical thing to do."

He wanted just to protect? Mary wondered skeptically. But Papa would tell her not to leap to conclusions. Just because she'd grown up watching her father being harassed and targeted by police didn't mean all lawmen were like that.

Papa would always point out gently, when she reacted with anger to police who came snooping by, or she found out there'd been yet another audit of his business by Internal Revenue, that being Sal Giordano's younger brother meant he would always be under more scrutiny than an ordinary person. He had chosen not to participate in the illegal operations his brother ran, but as the son of a family that had been involved in nefarious activities for generations, it wasn't unreasonable for the law to suspect he must be involved in some way.

Maybe not. But the anger and resentment she'd felt toward the police growing up had never lessened.

"All done, Miss Mary!" Bunny announced, setting down the mallet.

"What happens next?" Brice asked.

"I'll mix the potatoes with fresh rosemary and put them and the green beans in to roast. The chicken will be pan fried and doesn't take as long. I'll dredge it in flour and put it back in the fridge. Before we put everything in the oven, we need to go cut some rosemary for the potatoes. Should have done it while we were harvesting the tomatoes, but I forgot."

The disturbing presence of Brice McAllister at her elbow might have had something to do with her absentmindedness.

"Finished with the salad," the culprit-in-question announced.

"Thanks. I'll get out the olives, onions and peppers when we come back in." She hesitated, wondering if the next suggestion was a good idea or not. But darn, she wasn't going to give up the natural complement to her chicken dish just because there was an interloper present. "I usually put white wine in the chicken. Would you like a glass?"

"Only if you're having one."

Mary laughed, remembering. "Mama used to say it was impossible to cook without a glass of wine in hand. I have a nice Frascoti I'll open when we come back in."

Putting flour on a plate, she quickly coated the chicken pieces Bunny had pounded flat, put them in a dish, and set them back into the fridge. After one last dribble of oil over the beans and potatoes, she put them in the preheated oven to roast.

"Ready to cut the rosemary?"

"Yes!" Bunny said. "I love the smell when I run my fingers through it."

Very conscious of Brice walking beside her, she opened the door, trailing Bunny down the garden path to the rosemary bush, where Mary coached her to cut some sprigs before picking some basil and oregano leaves to add to the salad.

When they walked back in, she opened the oven to sprinkle the rosemary sprigs over the potatoes.

"Wow. That smells incredible," Brice said.

"See?" Bunny bounced on tiptoes. "I told you Miss Mary is a terrific cook."

"My mouth is watering already."

"Thank you both," she said, gratified. "Nothing a cook likes better than enthusiastic diners. Would you like some cheese, *mimmo*?"

"Yes, please!"

"Get your favorite crackers out of the pantry while I slice some cheese and pour the wine." After checking the potatoes, which were nearly done, she said, "It's about time to start the chicken. You can sit on your stool and watch, Bunny."

"Can I stir it?" Bunny asked as she went to the pantry to get the crackers.

"The chicken will be too hot, *mimmo*. It might pop and burn you while it's sautéing. You can put capers in a bowl for me to cook with the chicken." When she went to pull a bottle out of the wine cooler, Brice said, "I can open that if you like."

She handed him the bottle. "Thanks. There are wineglasses in the sideboard."

She took cheese from the fridge, her favorite Reggianno di Parmesan, some of the sharp white cheddar Bunny liked, a

Peccorino, and a blue, for variety, then plucked an apple from a bowl on the counter.

"You can cut that up, if you want."

"Sure thing."

He was used to being helpful, she had to give him that. And then smiled; her mama would have chased a man out of her kitchen with a carving knife, telling him cooking was woman's work. Whereas she and Ian had been happy to share kitchen chores. Her smile faded on a wave of sadness.

It had been a long time since she'd had a man in her kitchen. The sharp grief those memories still evoked just confirmed that she wasn't yet healed enough to move on.

No matter how much Brice McAllister made her senses tingle.

She handed him the packages of cheese and a clean knife. "Plates are in the sideboard too. Are you ready to hop up, *mimmo*?"

"Yes! I'm hungry!"

"Tell Uncle Brice to be quick with the cheese while you put the crackers in this bowl." As the little girl transferred handfuls of crackers into the bowl, Mary watched as McAllister sliced the cheese.

"Airplane coming in for landing!" he said, teasing Bunny with a slice as he moved it toward her mouth, then away. "No, had to wave off the landing. We'll try again. Coming in!" he said, this time popping the slice into her mouth between giggles.

He really was good with her, Mary thought. He obviously enjoyed teasing Bunny, but never to the point of frustrating or annoying the child. Despite herself, she felt a further easing of her wariness.

A deeply buried sense of caution immediately protested. Feeling less wary didn't mean she was ready to start dating, she countered the alarm. Even if he did make her senses fizz like expensive Italian mineral water.

He handed her a glass of wine. "You can officially begin cooking."

Nodding, she had to chuckle.

"See, I told you Uncle Brice would make you laugh!" Bunny cried.

"You were right. But you always are, aren't you, *mimmo*? Have some cheese and crackers. The rest of dinner will be ready soon."

She put olive oil in the pan and started sautéing the chicken. When it was browned and just tender, she stirred in the wine, capers, and lemon juice, cooked it another minute and then removed it from the heat, letting it sit in the pan as she got the potatoes and green beans out of the oven.

"Bunny, set the table while I put food in serving dishes?"

"Yes, Miss Mary. Uncle Brice, you can help."

Mary smiled as she watched the small girl direct the big man who towered over her to pull out silverware, plates, napkins and arrange them on the table. He walked over to fetch the wine and wineglasses, as well as Bunny's glass and water, and set everything on the table while Mary transferred chicken and vegetables to serving dishes.

Finally, she got the salad dressing from the fridge, along with olives, hot Italian peppers, radishes, and onions, and brought them to the table.

"You make your own salad dressing?" he asked, looking at the carafe.

"Of course. Olive oil, balsamic vinegar, and seasonings."

"Bet it's spectacular."

She motioned him to the table. "Shall we eat, and you can see?"

"Thanks again for cooking such a great meal for self-invited guests," he murmured.

She smiled. "Bunny knows she's welcome anytime." She paused. "Anyone she loves enough to call 'uncle' is welcome too."

Was he welcome? she wondered as she sat down. She'd just recently gotten her house fully furnished, her job mastered, and settled into a comfortable routine.

Probably not, she admitted to herself. Nice as he seemed to be, she didn't need an attractive man like Brice McAllister disturbing the tranquility of her new life.

And he was big enough, and compelling enough, to create a Texas-size disturbance.

Chapter Four

AFTER SPENDING A week back at his job in Austin, Brice decided to head to the Hill Country over the weekend. He could visit with his brothers, but also do a little more on his unofficial investigation about the problems on the Triple A. Poke around and look up some of the people who had recently sold land to Thomason. Chat them up and see if the real estate agent had made any mention of his plans for the property.

He'd also stop by to see Tom, Elaine and Bunny. And hopefully, their lovely neighbor.

He'd thoroughly enjoyed the evening he'd spent at the cottage and the meal had been terrific. Mary Williams was just as good a cook as Bunny had claimed. He'd appreciated her apology for her earlier unfriendliness, and though she continued to be cautious, she had opened up more. He'd learned that her mother had taught her to appreciate wine along with cooking. With her dark hair and eyes, he'd first thought she might be Hispanic, but by her choice of recipes and pet name for Bunny, he figured she must be of Italian descent.

Running the image of her through his mind, he felt a swell of desire. The wave of attraction that had swept him away when he saw her in that halter top and short shorts the first afternoon at Tom and Elaine's didn't diminish at their next meeting, when she was wearing that flattering cotton dress.

He was pretty sure the simmer of attraction was mutual. If it was, would she ignore it? Or eventually, when she grew to trust him, act on it?

That was an intriguing possibility.

He'd have to remind himself to take it slow. If she was attracted to him, the caution he'd already seen her display wouldn't be overcome easily. If he moved too fast or pressed too hard, she'd retreat.

He still had no idea where she'd come from. She might be from some other part of Texas, but if so, she'd never developed a regional accent. She spoke with Standard American pronunciation and might have grown up anywhere.

Most striking to him, except for one brief mention of her mother, was her otherwise total absence of reference to any family or friends before her arrival a year ago in Whiskey River. Something Elaine had mentioned to him too.

He also noted the shudder that had gone through her when Bunny talked about weapons. Maybe whoever she was avoiding from her previous life had threatened her with a firearm. Which meant she could be in real danger if the person showed up again.

He felt a swell of anger at the thought of anyone hurting her. Which made him more determined than ever to get her to trust him. If she was under threat from someone, he wanted to be the first person she'd call if the lowlife ever managed to track her down. He'd take great personal pleasure in dealing with a despicable piece of trash who would hurt a woman—especially this woman.

Though if she had been abused by a former lover, it was going to take a long time for another man to gain her trust.

When he thought of her beautiful dark eyes, that curvaceous body, and the intriguing hints her house and garden had given him of the character of the woman hidden behind that screen of caution, he knew the patience needed would be more than worth the effort.

He turned down the country road bordering Triple A land, then into a farm driveway which still had the "for sale" sign of Thomason's real estate firm planted near the road, a "sold" sticker slapped on top. Stuck in the ground beside the real estate post was a sign advertising "garage sale today."

Good, he thought. That meant the former owner, Jake Donaldson, whom he remembered vaguely from school as being half a dozen years older than him, would be home and he wouldn't have wasted the drive. Even better, with the yard sale going on, he could let Donaldson assume he'd come for that, which would make the man even more relaxed. There was something about having a Texas Ranger, even an off-duty one, asking questions that tended to make people nervous, even when they didn't need to be.

He parked his truck and walked over to the barn where tables set out in front were covered with an assortment of clothing, knickknacks, appliances, books and other things a family getting ready to move wanted to get rid of.

Fortunately, Donaldson himself was arranging things on one of the tables. Spotting him, the man gave Brice a nod and walked over to meet him. "Hey, Brice. Thanks for coming out. Not much of interest to you out here," he waved a hand toward the table, "but there are tools and things in the barn. Couple of chain saws, some auto mechanic equipment."

"You won't need them where you're moving?"

"No. We bought a house just outside San Antonio. Real suburban living. Got a good job for a construction firm located in the city."

"That why you decided to sell up?"

Donaldson shook his head. "I really decided long ago. Only held on to the ranch until Pa died. He worked all his life to keep this place afloat. Frankly, I don't want to work that hard."

"You know why Thomason wanted to buy it? He's not exactly a hardworking kind of guy."

Donaldson laughed disdainfully. "Shoot, no, he's more a 'let my assistant do it, because I might break a manicured fingernail' kind of guy. Always did have more money than sense. No idea why he wanted it—Pa did his damnedest, but he struggled to make a go of it. I can't imagine Thomason's got a buyer in mind who'd give him more for it than he paid us. It would be different if it were your family's place, with those high cliffs overlooking the river, a prime location for some rich city dude to build a weekend house."

No enlightenment to be had here, Brice thought regretfully. "I'll go take a look at those tools. Duncan might need some of that equipment out at the ranch."

Since Donaldson expected it, Brice walked into the barn and made a circuit around it. Melancholy filled him as he gazed at plows, feed troughs, harnesses, fencing, baling gear, and other accoutrements that said this had once been a working ranch.

He felt a renewed appreciation for all the work Duncan had put in over the years, hauling the Triple A back from the edge of bankruptcy and keeping it going.

No rich pretty-boy real estate agent was going to drive it into the ground now, he vowed.

Brice was about to walk back out of the barn when a vaguely familiar car came down the driveway. He stopped short, then a slow smile crept across his face as he watched Mary Williams shut down the engine and climb out. His smile deepened when he noted she was wearing another of those dark, shapeless dresses he'd seen that first day at the library. And sure enough, her hair was pulled back into the Old Maid Librarian bun, the thick glasses hiding her pretty eyes.

He watched as she greeted Donaldson politely, then wandered over to a table to look at an assortment of books. With a sense of anticipation, he strolled over to halt beside her.

"Bookshelves at home not full enough?"

He kicked himself for not coughing or clearing his throat first, for she jumped about a foot, her eyes widening with an alarm that made something twist in his chest. There was the odd robbery or assault from time to time, but Whiskey River was generally a pretty safe place to live. It hurt his heart to see that something had conditioned her to be so apprehensive.

"Sorry, I didn't mean to startle you."

"My fault," she said with an uncertain smile. "When it comes to books, I get absorbed pretty quickly. Lose all track of place and time. Becoming a librarian was my ideal occupation. I get to spend all day around books."

"I know lots of people read on tablets or their phones now. But there's something about the feel of a book in your hands, the smell of paper and binding."

She angled her head at him, surprised. "Yes, there is. Although I do a lot of reading on my phone—always have it with me, easier to read a few pages waiting in line at the grocery store or the take-out counter, or over lunch—I always like to have 'real' book waiting at home." She paused for a moment, then said, "I wouldn't have taken you for a reader."

"Because I'm a former football jock, and therefore barely literate?" he said wryly.

"Not at all. I'm sure football jocks are very literate. They have to read all those confusing diagrams with Xs and Os, don't they? I said that because you're in law enforcement. I would think lawmen were more action oriented, too impatient to sit still in one place and read a book."

"My reading habits might not be up to librarian standards, but I like a good book. Are you looking for anything in particular?"

"I don't collect first editions, if that's what you mean. Just . . . books. Since I moved here, I've been particularly interested in out-of-print books of stories, memoirs, guidebooks—anything about the area."

"Texas is a great place for legends and sayings."

"So I've become aware. Sometimes people coming into the library make a comment and I'm not really sure what they mean."

She smiled, the first time not with Bunny that she'd given him one of those open, genuine, terrifically appealing smiles. Delighted, Brice felt like he'd just won the lottery.

"One day, an old guy looking at records was irritated because he thought the county clerk had mixed up his tax account. 'The guy's so stupid,' he said, 'he's one bubble off plumb.' I had to get him to explain what he meant. I think he laughed about the dumb librarian for the rest of the day."

"You're being a little hard on yourself. There are probably lots of women who've never used a plumb level. For that matter, many of the younger generation probably haven't either, since these days you can use an app on your cell phone to check whether the shelf you're putting up is level."

"I imagine you've used a plumb level."

Brice nodded. "Growing up on the ranch, we learned to use all sorts of old tools. Money's always tight, so no need to buy anything newer if the one Granddaddy used still does the job. Have you found any gems here?"

"No, unfortunately. But Shirley told me about a local flea market, out on the rural road past Buddy's. I'm not exactly sure where that is, but I can probably find it."

"Old Man Tessel's place?"

She angled her head, eyes up, visibly scanning her memory, then nodded. "Yes, I think that was the name Shirley mentioned."

"I'm going to meet my brothers out at the Triple A later, so I'm headed that way. You can follow me if you want. Then you won't have to worry about getting lost. Phone GPS works well along the main roads, but with the hills and narrow valleys, coverage can get spotty pretty quick if you're on a back road."

He held his breath, waiting. He wasn't asking her to come along with him in the same vehicle, and he'd let her know he was heading on someplace else, so accepting his offer wouldn't be like inviting her to spend the day with him. He hoped it would be casual and unthreatening enough for her to accept.

Though he might wish he *could* spend a whole day with her, this would at least buy him a little more time.

After a moment, obviously thinking through the pros and cons, she nodded. "Yes, if it wouldn't be too much trouble. It's kind of you to offer."

"No trouble at all. As I said, I'm going that way anyway."

"Okay, thank you then."

"I'm parked over there. The gray truck. I'll wait for you to pull out behind me."

"Lead on."

After a word of goodbye to Donaldson, Brice turned toward his truck. Trying to keep a handle on his elation, he slowed his pace, not wanting to seem too eager. Though he was. Ridiculous to feel as delighted by her letting him lead her to a flea market as if she'd actually accepted a date.

Did he want to date her?

Well . . . maybe. Not only was she gorgeous, with a mysterious past that lit up all his protective instincts, but she also intrigued him. The discussion about Texas sayings confirmed his suspicions that she wasn't a native of the state.

What had brought her to the small town of Whiskey River?

Much as he was impatient to find out, everything about her shouted that she was a very private person who didn't welcome questions about her past. He'd have to be patient and learn about her bit by bit.

It was way too early to think about dating. They needed to get to know each other better first, see if there could be more between them than a simmering attraction. Somehow he knew, for her, physical attraction wouldn't be enough.

Keeping an eye on his rearview mirror, Brice drove off at a moderate pace. The back roads had a lot of twists and turns, going up rises to plateaus with broad vistas, then curving down to cross creek beds, dry this time of year, but which in winter or spring could flood suddenly in a heavy rain. Following someone in this area, if you didn't know the roads, could be dangerous if you drove too fast.

Half an hour later, they arrived at an old farmhouse known locally as "Old Man Tessel's." Part antique store, part salvage shop, part junktique, it and several other buildings beside it carried a varying and eclectic mix of merchandise, usually at bargain prices.

Brice pulled up into the lot, hopped out of his truck, and waited for Mary to park her vehicle beside his. "Thanks so much for the navigation help," she said as she got out of the car. "I don't think I could have found the place otherwise."

"There are easier ways to get here by the main roads, but it's faster by back roads if you know where you're going. Speaking of, do you know your way back to town from here?"

"I think so. Turn left out of the parking lot, head south for several miles, turn onto the highway to Johnson City, then straight back into town?"

"Right. It's all main—or relatively main—roads from here going that way, so you should be okay."

"Good. Thanks again."

Time for his next ploy. His pulse rate kicking up, he held his breath again as he checked his watch. "I have some time to kill before I meet my brothers. Would you mind if I tag along? Might find some books I'm interested in too."

He could see her retreat, the wariness returning to her face. "Suit yourself," she said, her tone noticeably cooler.

He'd expected that reaction, but at least she hadn't told him she would prefer it if he'd just leave. "If you see any tales of Texas, I can let you know if it's a good book or not. My brother Duncan collected most all of them he could find when we were younger."

"Will we run into 'Old Man Tessel'?" she asked, looking at the sign.

Brice laughed. "I'm not sure whether there ever was such a person—maybe he's just another Texas legend. The place is run by Polly Winstead and her sister Meg now. Polly renovates houses, so she's always coming across architectural odds and ends, and Meg makes a living finding things at yard and estate sales she can resell here."

"Sounds fascinating."

"After you."

They walked in, Brice waving to Polly, who was in the little central area that served as an office, garbed in her usual uniform of paint-splashed overalls, stripping the finish off an old piece of furniture. "Hey, Brice, how are you?"

"Can't complain. And you?"

"Always something in town that needs fixing or renovating, so I'm fine."

"Polly, have you met Mary Williams? She's the reference librarian at the Whiskey River library."

"No, I haven't. Welcome! I'd shake your hand, but I've got paint thinner on my gloves. You folks looking for anything in particular?"

"Books, mostly," Mary said. "Although I also collect old kitchen things."

"Books are in the next room—the 'library,' we call it. You're in luck about the kitchen things. Meg's found some great items recently at estate sales. She's set it all out in the old kitchen, on the other side of the library."

"We'll find it. Thanks, Polly."

"You're welcome, Brice. Nice to meet you, Mary."

"And you, Polly."

"What are you looking for?" Mary asked as they walked toward the book display, a hefty trace of suspicion in her voice.

"Old Zane Grey westerns. Anything by Larry McMurtry. Bios and legends about Texas Rangers. I'll help you find some Texas lore. If you're going to live here, you need to be educated about it. And about Texas expressions. So your library customers don't need to explain themselves."

"You going to start my education?"

"I could if you like."

She angled a glance at him. Pleased, Brice knew he'd intrigued her. Intrigued her enough to let him tag along a while longer?

"Okay," she said as they walked into the room whose rows of books on shelves and laid out on tables justified Polly's description of "library." "Tell me your favorite Texas expression. I'll see if I can figure it out."

"Just one?" He shook his head. "That's tough. There are so many good ones."

She smiled, further encouraging him. "Start with one."

After thinking for a minute, Brice said, "I used to use this one when I wanted to annoy my brothers. It would really make them mad, because I'm the youngest, so they always thought they could do everything better than me. It was especially effective when they were bragging about how well they were going to do something."

He paused. She waited, definitely interested now. "And . . ."

"'You couldn't hit the floor if you fell out of bed.'"

To his delight, she giggled. "I like it."

He swept her a bow. "No extra charge."

Disarmed now, she had relaxed, making no further protest as they both rummaged through the books on the table and browsed those on the shelves. Brice had no luck locating any westerns of interest, but Mary picked up an old tourist guide. "Some of these places might not even exist any longer," she said, thumbing through it, "but it will be fun visiting the ones that do. Well, I'm off to check out the kitchen gear. Thanks again for your help."

"I'm going to take a look too." Before, frowning, she could voice the protest he could see she wanted to utter, he added quickly, "I think I mentioned my sister-in-law does interior design? She makes lamps out of teacups and various other kitchen gear. If I find anything interesting, I'll get it for her."

Appearing mollified, Mary let him walk along with her to the kitchen. Stopping short on the threshold, she uttered a gasp of delight.

The room really was the original farmhouse kitchen, complete with original sink, an old refrigerator that looked like it was from the '50s, with a farm table in the center surrounded by old chairs. Not a working kitchen, though, since every surface was covered by tools, linens, pots, pans, and other items.

"It's wonderful!" she breathed, heading over immediately to check out the linens.

Brice browsed through the gear set out on the table, unable to identify most of it. Picking up a long wooden item that looked like a piece of log with the ends flattened off and center scooped out, he said, "Do you know what this is for?"

Mary looked up. "It's a dough bowl. For making bread."

"Are you sure?" He picked it up and put it on his head.

"Kinda looks like one of those old fore-and-aft Navy hats. Or maybe Napoleon's. You know, the one he wears in the paintings when he's standing like this." Brice straightened, made his face look stern, and stuck one hand into his shirt.

To his surprise, Mary burst out laughing. So she did have a sense of humor after all, he thought, grinning.

"You look ridiculous. Take that bowl off your head."

"Dunno. Abby—my sister-in-law—might make something out of it. Put candles in the hollowed-out part and surround them with old lasso rope. I think I'll get it."

He picked up another item, one that had a long patterned handle like a piece of silverware, but ended in a comb-like piece with the tines about four inches long. "What's this?"

"A cake breaker. You use it to cut cakes that are delicate and might squish if you tried to cut them with a regular knife."

"Looks like it might be a comb for someone with really thick hair."

"Don't comb your hair with it!" she cried before grinning, he put it back down.

She gave him a reproving look, but unrepentant, he picked up another item. "This tin box? Almost rectangular, but long and narrow. Ah, I know! It must be used to store a football." He gave her an innocent look. "No?"

"How about a tin to store your freshly made loaf of bread," she said dryly.

He shook his head. "Naw, I think it would be better for the football. Sure could have used something like this during practice on a rainy day, to keep the ball drier. What about this?" He held up a metal implement with a long handle that ended in a large semicircular, slotted piece of metal. "A masher for very large potatoes?"

By now, having caught on to the game, she couldn't help smiling. "It's a pot strainer. You put it on the top of your pot in place of a lid, then tip the pot to drain off liquid. Useful when cooking vegetables."

Keeping a straight face, Brice picked up several more items. Proposing some outlandish use for them, then looking to her to correct him, kept her chuckling while she chose some linens and several glasses made of cobalt-blue Depression glass.

"How do you know about all this old stuff?"

"My *nonna* taught me how to cook. She had a lot of utensils like these."

Inspecting the blue glasses she'd set aside, he said, "Those are real pretty. How about this to go with them?" He pointed to a deep-blue glass container that looked like a cookie jar with a lid. "The surface of the glass looks like lace."

Mary looked at it and sighed. "Gorgeous! It is lace—the pattern's called 'Royal Lace,' and it's one of the most expensive types of cobalt-blue Depression glass. The piece is in perfect condition. I hate to even think what it must cost."

After hesitating, she said, "What the heck," picked up the price tag and read it, then shuddered. "Bad as I thought."

"How much?"

"Two hundred dollars. Which is still a good deal; in an antique shop, it might be a hundred dollars more. But that's not in the budget. Maybe I'll put it on my Christmas-for-me list."

Her body language said she was ready to leave. Figuring he'd dragged out the time she'd allow him to spend with her about as long as he could, he glanced at his watch again. "I'd better be heading out. Need me to carry the items out for you?" Then he quickly held up a hand. "Sorry, automatic response when in the company of a lady. I know you can handle it."

"I can manage, but thanks." But this time, she didn't seem unfriendly when she turned him down.

They walked together back to the office, paid Polly for their items, then headed back out to their vehicles.

"Thanks again for your help," Mary said as she stowed her purchases in her car.

"Anytime. Sure you know how to get back to town?"

"Yes, I don't think I'll get lost."

"If you do, text Tom or Elaine. A text message will go through when a call won't."

"I'll keep that in mind."

"If Tom isn't sure how to find you, he has backup." He gave her a grin. "He can call out a Texas Ranger."

She gave him an exasperated look. "Goodbye, Brice McAllister."

"Goodbye, Mary Williams."

She bent to get into her car, paused, and looked back at him over her shoulder. "Bunny was right. You do make me laugh."

Pleased, Brice smiled to himself as he climbed up into his truck. Then sat and watched Mary settle herself in the car, fasten her seat belt and drive off.

He felt this odd, inexplicable sense of protest at watching her drive away, as if it were wrong for her to leave him.

Still, he felt pleased about the progress he'd made today. She was relaxing more around him. And he wasn't above using Bunny to make her feel even more comfortable.

Because if anything did happen to frighten or threaten her, he wanted her to be one to call out this Texas Ranger.

Chapter Five

LOOKING OUT AT the eager faces, Mary turned another page of the book. "Then the Prince arrived and helped the Princess fight off the dragon, who ran away, howling." She made a howling noise, setting the children to giggling. "The Prince and Princess put away their swords and went off to get ice cream, and lived happily ever after. The end."

"Yeah!" Bunny said, clapping with the other children.

"You tell the bestest stories, Miss Mary," another little girl said.

"That's because I have the bestest listeners. Okay, that's all for today." She stood up from her stool in the middle of the semicircle, the gaggle of children around her standing, too, as their parents come in to claim them, thank her, and bid her goodbye. "See you soon, Miss Mary," Bunny said, holding Elaine's hand as they walked out.

Mary smiled as the children headed down the hallway and out the front door. She'd been hesitant at first, but she was glad now that Shirley had talked her into doing a story hour for children at the library. She loved watching the eager faces, avidly listening, ready to believe every tale, no matter how fantastical. Was there anything sweeter than the absolute trust of a child?

She enjoyed each of them and would not allow herself to be sad. She might not ever have one of her very own to love, but all the children she encountered could do with a little more affection. She would spread all the affection she had to share with these, with some extra reserved just for Bunny.

Story time concluded at three o'clock. After the emotional high of spending time with children, she usually went home early, letting the glow last. Since it had been particularly hot today, she'd treat herself to a stop by the Diner. She must be becoming a real Texan, she thought as she gathered up her things, because she'd developed a strong preference for sweet iced tea, and the Diner made the best in town.

The idea of becoming a real Texan made her think of Brice McAllister, his Texas sayings, and his nonsensical uses for the kitchen items he'd found. He had made her smile. He was, she conceded, as Elaine had promised, a very engaging guy.

With whom to be casually acquainted.

She could have walked to the Diner, but since she was on her way home, she drove over. After parking in front, she strolled in, seeing the usual gaggle of ranchers and farmers seated at the far tables. Most of them retired, but a few still actively running their spreads, the group gathered in the late afternoons almost every weekday to chew the fat and talk about ranching.

To her surprise, she noted Brice McAllister sitting with them. Spotting her, as well, he gave her a nod.

A wave of uncertainty rippled through her. She couldn't pretend now that she hadn't seen him. Would he come over to talk with her? Did she want him to?

She had to admit, she'd enjoyed the time at the flea market. She'd felt . . . more comfortable around him. But that didn't mean she would feel comfortable being around him too often.

She wasn't ready for that yet with any man. She might never be.

After nodding back, she went over to the counter to order her tea. She wasn't trying to eavesdrop, but the ranchers' conversation carried easily to where she stood, waiting for the server to fill her order.

"Haven't seen any strangers around lately," one of the older men said, evidently responding to a question Brice had asked. "Duncan asked us a while back to be on the lookout, when his wife first had difficulties on the ranch. Saw some folks in a truck nobody knew back then, but nothing since."

"Thomason mention to anyone what he wanted to do with the land he's buying up?"

"Silver spoon he was born with had a teaspoon of honey in it too," one of the ranchers said. "He's always talking big about some fantastic deal he's putting together."

"That boy thinks the sun comes up to hear him crow," another said.

"After Jernigan sold out to him, he told me he asked Thomason if he was going to put cattle back on the land," the first man added. "Thomason said why 'deal with animals that are hardly worth spit in a good year?' Said he'd stock something better than that."

"Cutting horses bring a good penny, but can't see him competing with the Kellys when it comes to horse breeding," Brice said. "Did he mention anything else?"

"Not that I heard," the first man said. "Boy's town-bred, wouldn't know the first thing about training horses. He'd have to hire someone, and there's nobody around better than the Kellys."

"Any of you hear anything, you let me know, okay?" Brice said.

"Sure, Brice. You take care of yourself, now. We were right sorry to hear about your friend, Trooper Martin, God rest his soul. Good man."

"He was. Y'all take care too."

Brice got up, and after tipping his hat to the men, walked toward her. Another wave of nervousness went through her. Should she smile and engage him in conversation? Or nod pleasantly and look the other way?

Watching him walk over out of the corner of her eye, she felt the same jolt of attraction that she'd felt the other times he'd come near her. That intense, impossible-to-ignore aura of masculinity that called out to everything female in her.

The look in his eyes that told her he found her attractive

too.

She'd probably at least have to greet him. She didn't want him to think she was encouraging his interest, but she'd been rude before and he didn't deserve that, especially after he had gone out of his way to be helpful.

"Ah, I see the Diner has converted you to their sweet tea," he said as the young woman brought over her order. "I think I'll get a refill myself," he said, handing his cup to the server "Fill my to-go cup up if you will, Sally Ann?"

"Sure, Brice. Anything you want. Anything," Sally Ann added, batting her eyes.

He just smiled—not ignoring the flirtatious gesture, but not encouraging it to go further, either.

It was silly of her to find the girl's blatant interest . . . annoying. Of course women were interested in him. Brice McAllister was over six foot of handsome, virile, charming male.

She could appreciate that without being in the market herself.

"Heading back to the library?" he asked.

"No, I go home early after I do story hour on Mondays."

"Story hour? Bet you're good at that. Bunny says you tell great stories, not all of them from books. That she can give you a character and you can make up stories for her."

She paused while the server came back with his tea refill. "Thanks much, Sally Ann," he said, giving her another easy smile.

"Just for you, Brice."

Mary found herself annoyed again—until Brice gave her a quick glance and rolled his eyes. She had to bite her lip to keep from laughing out loud.

"Headed home? I'll walk you out."

"Is there something wrong?" she found herself blurting as they walked out. "I couldn't help but overhear, and you seemed to be interrogating those gentlemen."

"Not interrogating. Folks around here want to know what's happening with their neighbors, so they can help them out if necessary. My brothers have had some trouble on the ranch, small incidents, but together they add up to making it harder to run the ranch at a profit. A local real estate agent has been buying up land around the borders of the ranch. The local rich boy, son of an important family, who tried to lord it over everyone when we were at school. We don't like him, and the feeling is mutual. If it were anyone else buying the land, we might not think anything of it. But knowing how much bad blood there is between us and Thomason . . ."

Mary frowned. Brice McAllister might be helpful, but maybe he was more like the harassing police she'd known than she'd originally thought. "You're investigating him when he hasn't done anything? Isn't that . . . unethical?"

"Nothing unethical about asking questions. I wouldn't begin a full-on investigation unless I turn up evidence of wrongdoing, and I don't have any yet. At least, nothing solid that can be proven. So . . . I keep asking questions."

"Do you always ask so many questions?" she demanded, her tone sharper than she'd intended.

He smiled. "I reckon I do. I'm just naturally curious, especially if things don't seem to add up. I don't mean to be intrusive, though."

"Sorry, I'm a bit sensitive on that point. I'm . . . very private myself, so if I see someone pestering people with questions, I tend to feel that they are being . . . harassed."

His smile faded. "I'd never want to do that," he said seriously, holding the door open for her to walk out. "My stepmom, Miss Dorothy, would give me a licking with a hickory branch if she thought I was bothering someone."

"Good to know." Could she believe him? Whether she could or not, now that she'd blundered into displaying her sensitivity on that point, it was time to change the subject. "Did your sister-in-law like the bread bowl?"

His smile was back, making her feel better. He didn't want to be thought as harassing—but she didn't like to think of herself as churlish. "She even liked my suggestion for what she might do with it. Makes me feel . . . validated. Like maybe I'm not hopeless at design after all. You really ought to visit her shop. I think you'd like it—might even find some inspiration there."

"Maybe I will." She'd need the sun to go down for a few more hours before it would be comfortable enough to do any weeding in the garden. "How late is her shop open?"

"Until six. After their marriage, Abby moved into the cabin she helped my brother Grant refurbish—an even better example of her style than the shop, not to mention it sits on the prettiest hilltop in three counties. Maybe I could show you it sometime."

"Maybe," she said noncommittally. "What did you say the shop's address was?"

He held out his hand in a wait-a-minute gesture. "I don't mean to seem pushy but . . . it's on another of those back country roads, pretty hard to find if you don't know the area. And honestly, it also happens to be in the direction of the Triple A, where I'm meeting my brothers again for dinner. Might be better if you follow me out—"

"So I won't get lost, reliant only on a text message that might fail, resulting in the need to call out a Texas Ranger?" she finished, giving him a suspicious look. "If it's that hard to find, why did she open a shop there?"

By now they'd reached her car, and still watching him, she clicked open the lock.

He halted beside her. "When she first came to Whiskey River, a pregnant widow short on funds, she rented an old ranch house that was inexpensive because it's in the middle of nowhere, down an old dirt road off the highway a ways out of town. She started furnishing it with castoffs she picked up off the side on the road, in thrift shops, and found materials she turned into something else. Like an old cedar stump whose roots she braided with mini-LED lights and turned into a chandelier. Painted colanders made into lampshades. Interesting, innovative, completely different from anything you'd find in a store. Friends who visited the house saw them and started asking her to make them something similar. Then her mother-in-law, her late husband's mother, a huge admirer of her designs, urged her to start an online store. Eventually she turned the garage next to the house into a shop and showroom. By then, she was well enough known online and in town that people were willing to make the drive."

She'd intended to tell him goodbye and drive off, but she had to admit, the shop intrigued her in spite of herself. "Okay, sold. I think I need to see this for myself."

"Are you willing to let me lead you?" Her eyes must have widened at that double entendre, for once again, he held out a hand. "Sorry, that didn't come out right."

"I'm not willing to be led," she said pointedly. "But you can show me the way to the shop."

Looking relieved, he said, "Good. I'll introduce you to Abby. I think you'll like her. Like you, she's shy, not good with strangers. Had an overbearing mother who belittled her all her life. You won't believe this after you've seen what she creates, but she grew up with her mother denigrating her 'crude little craft projects' and telling her she had no talent and would never make anything of herself. Boy, has she proved that woman wrong."

"Good for her," Mary said, feeling an immediate sympathy for the designer. "I think I will like her."

"Ready? Let's hit the road. Before we go, here's another Texas saying. Now, being a high-class city woman from a ritzy neighborhood in Dallas, Abby's mother would never have described the trash Abby transforms like this, but if she were to use a countrified expression, she would say they started out as 'useless as two buggies in a one-horse town.'"

Mary smiled at the image. "I think I like Texas-isms. And women who can make something of two buggies in a one-horse town."

"Follow me, then, round two."

IT WAS PROBABLY good that she had followed Brice, Mary thought, as they finally approached the modest ranch house located on a dirt road after they'd turned off a small county road that was hardly larger. The exterior of the house was neat as a pin, the terrace in front boasting a table and chairs separated from the road by an attractive bed planted with lantanas, cactus, and prairie grasses interspersed with wrought-iron sculptures. His sister-in-law's work?

Brice pulled his truck to a stop in front of a building beside the ranch house, which looked like the converted garage he had described, while an old wooden sign over the entry door announced "Hidden Treasures."

By the time she pulled in beside him and got out of her

car, Brice had already hopped down from his truck and was striding over to meet a tall, slim blond woman who emerged from the shop. He gave her a hug and they both turned to Mary as she walked down the terrace toward them.

"Abby, let me introduce Mary Williams, the reference librarian in town. She lives in the cottage next door to my good friends, Elaine and Tom. Bunny invited me into her house—" He gave Mary a grin while Abby groaned.

"I can believe that. My daughter, Katie, would do the same thing. Kids—they have no sense of privacy or decorum."

"It makes them charming, though," Mary said. "That innocent sense that all the people *they* like must obviously like each other too."

"Exactly," Abby said wryly.

"The décor in her cottage is eclectic," Brice continued. "Old collectables mixed with new pieces, so I thought she'd enjoy seeing your work. Mary, my sister-in-law and fabulous designer, Abby McAllister."

"Delighted to meet you," Mary said.

"The same. Would you like to look around the shop? I'd be happy to tell you about any of the pieces that interest you. If you are a craftsperson, too, I can give you directions on how to make some of the things for yourself."

"That would be kind of you!" Mary said, impressed. Abby must care about clients, not just income, if she were willing to pass along trade secrets rather than hold out for a sale. She already felt she'd met a kindred spirit.

"I'll leave y'all to it. Another Texas saying for you before I go, Mary. You and Abby have 'howdied, but you've not shaken,' so time to get better acquainted."

Abby laughed. "Texas. Isn't it great?"

Mary nodded. "I'm beginning to agree."

"Grant, you're coming out to the ranch for dinner?"

"Yes, it's my last night here. I head to Johnson City tomorrow."

"Case-related?" When he nodded, Abby said, "Okay. I know better than to ask what for. You'll probably get to the ranch before I do. You should stop by and see the renovations Grant's started on in the barn on the Scott place."

Abby turned to Mary. "When my husband's brother Duncan married Harrison Scott, whose father bought part of the original Triple A ranch when the family had to sell some land during hard times, they reunited the property. Since Harrison moved into the McAllister ranch house, that left the house her father built and some of the barns empty. As a former Marine, Grant had the idea that it could become a great venue to host events—days out for kids at base daycares in San Antonio, riding events for recovering wounded vets, like he once was."

"She's too modest," Brice said. "Grant says the idea of using the Scott place to generate income, rather than having it stand idle or worse, selling off that section of the ranch, started with Abby. She's a great repurposer."

"Grant's just started on the work. He and Duncan are waiting for their small business loan to be approved."

"Sounds like it would be a good addition to the area," Mary said.

"Grant intends to do most of the grunt labor himself, in the time he can spare from mowing, fence repair and tending cattle. I'll see you later then, Brice."

"Thanks for showing me the way," Mary said.

"My pleasure. See you at dinner, Abby."

As he walked back to his truck, Mary struggled to prevent herself from sinking into melancholy. It was both warming—and painful—to observe how close Brice's family was, evident in his questioning to try to find out if someone was trying to harm the family ranch, in how enthusiastic an advocate he was for his sister-in-law's business, and in the obvious warmth and affection between them.

The blessing of family. Once, she had been blessed like that too. She still missed it keenly. She was still bitter over its destruction, a bitterness she might never overcome.

"Would you like some lemonade?" Abby was saying. "My daughter, Katie, makes great lemonade. You could enjoy a glass while you look around the shop."

"Are you sure there's time? I don't want to keep you late."

"It's just a hop, skip and a jump up a back road to the farmhouse. We have plenty of time. Katie will be excited to show someone new her lemonade-making skills."

Walking to the door of the ranch house, she opened it and called inside. A moment later, a lovely little girl of about six came running to the threshold. "Oh, you have a customer! I was playing a game and didn't hear anyone drive up."

"A thirsty customer. Mary, meet my daughter, Katie."

"Hi, Katie. It's nice to meet you."

"You're so pretty!" Katie said. At a reproving look from her mother, she added, "Well, she is, even if maybe it's not polite to say so."

Charmed, Mary said, "Thank you, Katie. And you are beautiful too."

"That's what my grandmother says when she wants me to wear one of the frilly dresses she buys me." The girl wrinkled her nose. "I like my pants and T-shirts better."

"Well, it wasn't polite, but at least it was a compliment," Abby said, shaking her head. "Do you think you could bring Miss Mary some of the lemonade you made this afternoon?"

"I would love to taste it. Your mommy says it's really special."

Katie nodded wisely. "It is. I'll bring some right out. Are you going to look at my mommy's shop? She makes so many pretty things. You'll probably want a teacup lamp. Mommy made me a pink one for my bedroom. It's my favoritest thing—except for riding my pony with Daddy."

"Off with you then, before she dies of thirst," Abby said.

Giggling, Katie ran back into the house.

"She is adorable!" Mary said, trying to tamp down the

inevitable flood of envy. "What a charmer."

Abby laughed, shaking her head. "Six, going on twenty-six. Thank heavens for Grant! She worships him and listens to him much better than she does to me. Otherwise, I'd be terrified of the thought of her becoming a teenager. Let's go into the shop and get out of the heat."

As they walked into the cool, air-conditioned building, Mary stopped short, not only for the blessed relief from the sun, but in absolute delight. "I hardly know where to look first!"

Abby shrugged modestly. "Take your time. I'm happy to tell you about—or give you construction details for—anything you see."

Mary wandered around, marveling at the tree-root chandelier Brice had mentioned, which was much more attractive than the mental picture she'd formed when he described it. The airy structure of tree roots threaded through with tiny LED lights both gave homage to the native trees of the area and to the shape and design of a traditional chandelier. On one wall, ladders formed bookcases; on another, beside a farm table, in an old buffet that had been stripped and whitewashed, rake heads removed from their handles served as a wineglass rack. But what particularly caught her eye were the old kitchen items made into lights—colanders and rectangular graters painted bright colors, with light bulbs inside providing illumination; green- and clear-glass canning jars with bulbs inside hung from chains to make pendant lighting over a kitchen peninsula.

And, of course, the famous teacup lamp Katie had described, a feminine fancy that would look wonderful on her bedside table.

When Katie came back, they sat at the farm table and sipped lemonade—which was indeed special, made out of fresh lemons she squeezed herself with one of her mother's old juice-squeezers, Katie told her.

"Well, I definitely need a teacup lamp," Mary said.

"I told you, you would!" Katie said triumphantly. "Nobody makes nicer things than my mommy."

Many of the items were more primitive than her style. But others were clever and, as Brice had suspected, inspiring.

"I'll start with a teacup lamp. I also love the lights you've made from kitchen items. I may have to ask you to teach me how to make some of them before I spend my whole month's salary."

"Can't have you blowing your salary on furnishings and starving to death," Abby said with a laugh. "One teacup lamp, then. I've got a supply of cups in my workshop, so you can pick your favorite colors and designs. Now, tell me what you'd like to make for yourself."

"It's hard to choose. I love the colander-and-grater lamps, but I think first, I'd like to make canning-jar lights to hang over my kitchen island."

"Do you have some canning jars?"

"No old ones. But I'd be willing to sacrifice some I already have and buy more to do tomatoes and peppers later in the season."

"You put up vegetables?"

"Yes. My grandmother did. The cottage I'm renting in Whiskey River is the first time I've had a yard large enough to grow enough vegetables to have extra to jar. I'm especially excited to make my grandmother's tomato relish."

"Sounds delicious. How about we make a deal? You bring jars to the shop and I'll show you how to make them into pendant lights. I'll buy some of your produce and you can show me how to make tomato relish."

"You don't have to buy it—I'll give you some. And yes, it's a deal."

Sipping the tart-sweet lemonade, smiling at the beautiful child, Mary felt better than ever about her decision to settle in Whiskey River. Brice told her Abby's mother had denigrated her talent? The woman was an idiot. Abby was a creative genius.

Along with warmth toward this woman she thought would become a friend, Mary felt a renewed appreciation for Brice McAllister. Who not only had been helpful—he'd understood her well enough to suspect she'd find a kindred spirit in Abby McAllister.

She hadn't really wanted him tagging along with her at the flea market, but she had to admit, she'd enjoyed his company. It had been a long time since she'd been around someone who made her laugh.

Especially a good-looking man.

Then, he'd led her here, introduced her to Abby, and left. Not crowding her. Not asking intrusive questions. Just open, friendly, helpful.

She'd had ample evidence from Elaine's testimony and her own eyes that he was indeed "one of the good guys."

Maybe she needed to be a little more open and friendly herself. And let herself enjoy more of his company if and when she encountered him.

Moving here wasn't about denying herself, but about starting fresh, without the chains that bound her to a past that had dragged her down.

Maybe, like the red hawks gliding in the blue, blue sky above the shop, she should try stretching out her wings and soaring a bit.

Chapter Six

THE FOLLOWING WEEKEND, Brice set out on the drive from Austin back to Whiskey River for the high school homecoming weekend. Most of the town came out for the football game, and a lot of alumni now living in towns scattered across Texas returned for it too. He expected to see a number of his former football teammates and band members, though it was not an official reunion year for his class.

Plus, he just enjoyed a chance to watch the game. He'd loved playing himself, and never lost his taste for 'Friday Night Lights,' the chief beginning-of-the-weekend entertainment in the fall for countless small towns in Texas.

Homecoming weekend added a few extra activities, with a picnic and barbecue Saturday in the town square. Reunion classes usually set up tents, booths with artists and vendors selling fall items, and face-painting, games and other activities for kids. Duncan and Grant would finish up ranch chores early enough to attend the tail end of the picnic, as would Elaine, Tom and Bunny.

Brice was hoping during one of the homecoming activities to have a chance to see Mary Williams.

Shaking his head with exasperation, he recalled the faux pas of his double entendre at the Diner after she'd confirmed her interest in visiting Abby's shop, when he'd asked if she were willing to let him lead her. He'd about bitten off his tongue, hoping he hadn't ruined all progress he'd made at the flea market in getting her to relax around him. But after an initial withdrawal, she'd pointedly replied that he could show her the way—leaving the choice of whether or not to follow up to her.

At least she'd allowed him to show her. Ah, there were so many things he'd like to show her!

Like how much he wanted to kiss her. Unfortunately, she was likely far from ready for that lesson.

He needed to stay patient and concentrate first on gaining enough of her trust that he could be confident she'd call on him for assistance if she were threatened. It made him sick to think that someone out there somewhere might have evil intentions toward her. More than anything else, at least for now, if such a person ever turned up, he wanted her to not hesitate for a second before calling him for advice.

And once she trusted him? Elaine might term him a "player," which he admitted he had been in his wilder youth, but the last several years, he'd preferred getting to know a woman and keeping company with the same one, until he or the lady decided they needed to move on. Or were forced to move on, he thought, frowning, his hurt and anger over his former girlfriend Ashley's betrayal stinging anew.

So, gain Mary's trust first. Then, if they both wanted it, maybe move on to something more than being mere acquaintances. He might not be ready for marriage, but he'd be more than ready to try a casual, longer-term relationship.

Elaine and Tom were great neighbors to her. He sensed that Abby would make her a good friend too. Another resource—if something or someone menacing showed up.

While attending the homecoming activities, he'd also see if he could turn up any more clues about what 'something big' that snake Thomason had planned for the property he was buying up.

Brice had left Austin in time to arrive before the football game started, so the pregame festivities were just about to begin when he pulled his truck into the hometown side's parking lot. He bought a ticket, a corn dog and some chili cheese fries at the concession stand, then headed up to the grandstand, looking to meet Duncan, Harrison, Grant, Abby and Katie. While he paused at the bottom of the steps, scanning the crowd to find his family, a skitter of excitement went through him. Sitting beside Abby, in an attractive cotton dress with a short sweater, was Mary Williams.

Talk about two birds and one stone, he thought, grinning as he climbed the metal steps.

Abby spotted him halfway up and waved. "Hi, Brice! You're just in time. The introduction of the Homecoming Royal Court is about to begin."

After greetings all around, Duncan said to Mary, "Back

when we were in high school, they would crown a homecoming queen and king at a high school dance on Saturday night. Kids nowadays, being more cosmopolitan and inclusive, instead of princesses, a queen and a king, the student body nominates a 'royalty court' that can include any ten students the kids think are the most helpful and influential in the school." He laughed. "Though as a former homecoming king, Brice probably regrets the passing of that ritual."

"Naw, I'm not that much of a dinosaur," Brice objected. "Observing more Texas traditions, Mary?"

Abby patted Mary on the shoulder. "I persuaded her that if she wanted to get to know Texas, she had to come to Friday night high school football. I told her it's a regional tradition and almost the whole town turns out for the home games, even when it's not Homecoming weekend."

Mary looked around. "Grade school kids playing tag behind the stands, parents of players huddled behind the benches, young couples with babies, old folks—it really is a cross section of everyone from town."

"But I think she really came so she could chat with Katie," Abby said.

"Mommy wouldn't let me bring lemonade, even though mine is better than what they sell. She said I had to buy it at the concession stand, to help the high school."

"That's right," Grant said. "Chili cheese fries and corn dogs," he continued, pointing to Brice's refreshments. "How many millions did Miss Dorothy cook for the Booster Club when you were playing high school football?"

"Millions, for sure. I used to think, sitting on the bench while the defense was on the field, how great they smelled."

"She always saved a batch for you for after the game, though."

"That she did. What a fine woman."

Brice sat down beside Katie and Mary. "Do you follow professional football?" he asked Mary.

"No. Actually, I don't know much about football."

Putting down his cheese fries, Brice clapped a hand to his heart. "Don't know about football! Sweetheart, we better school you up quick. Not understanding football could get you run out of Texas."

"Start her out easy," Duncan advised. "Save discussion of shotgun formations, veer defense, and running a skinny post for later."

Mary looked at him blankly. "Those are plays, I assume?"

Brice and Duncan looked at each other. "This is more serious than I thought. You better get started immediately," Duncan said.

"Why don't you tell me what you already know, and I'll fill in some of the gaps?" Brice said.

"There are two teams. Offense and defense. The quarterback gets the ball on offense and tries to make plays. The team with the ball wants to move it down the field across the goal line and score a touchdown. The team on defense wants to stop them."

"Okay, that's a start. Since the quarterback is key to the offense, the type of play a team runs usually depends on his best skill set. If he's an excellent passer, they'll do more passing plays. If he's a better runner than passer, they'll do a mix with more handoffs to running backs, or 'quarterback keepers,' where he runs the ball himself. And as you said, the job of the defense is to stop them from making plays. Once the game starts, I can explain as it goes along."

By the end of that long speech, Mary was staring at him. "You're really serious about this."

"Sweetheart, this is Texas. Football *is* serious business here. As is supporting the cheerleaders by chanting the cheers with them and singing the school song at the end of the game."

She looked at him like he'd been out in the heat too long. "Right."

For the first and second quarters, Brice explained the plays. Initially looking indifferent, as the game went on, she began to catch the crowd's excitement, and her questions became more enthusiastic.

At halftime, while the marching band took the field for their performance, Katie and Abby went off to get a hot dog and some fries.

"Remind me which position you played?" Mary asked.

"Right or left offensive guard. You'll remember the one in the middle of the line who hikes the ball—that's the center. The players on either side of him are the tackles, the players outside them are the guards. Their job is to block the defenders trying to get to the quarterback before he can throw the ball or hand it off to a running back."

"That's right—you told me before, the guard protects the play."

"Or the players."

"Keeping them safe."

"Exactly. It's kind of a badge of honor among guards and tackles to have your quarterback finish a game without getting grass stains on his uniform. Course, frustrating defenders who are trash-talking you and breathing curses in your face is fun too."

She laughed. "Protect your teammates, annoy the opposition?"

He smiled. "That's right. Annoyed and angry people sometimes get over-aggressive, out of position, or just plain forget what they're supposed to be doing."

"So you have lots of tactics up your sleeve."

"Many weapons make speedy work."

"I thought it was many hands make light work," she said dryly.

"That too."

"Hey, Brice! I hoped I'd see you here."

He looked up to see one of his former football teammates waving, then weaving through the crowd toward them. "Hey, Trey. Good to see you," Brice said as the man halted beside them.

"Good to see you, too." Trey angled his gaze down at Mary with a questioning look.

Responding to the unspoken request, Brice said, "Mary Williams, this is Trey Grayson, who played quarterback my first two years in high school. Trey, Mary's the reference librarian at the town library and our teammate, Tom Edgerton's, neighbor."

After they nodded and exchanged 'nice to meet yous,' Mary said, "You're the one whose jersey Brice tried to keep free of grass stains."

Trey laughed. "That's right. He did a fair job for an underclassman. A much better one with my successor. Made all-state his junior and senior year. Harley Dodson got very few grass stains on his jersey."

"What are you up to lately?" Brice asked.

"I drive back pretty much every weekend. My nephew is the quarterback now. I've seen you around town a few times, not close enough to hail. You've been back more often lately haven't you?" The look he gave Brice over Mary's head indicated he thought she might be the reason.

"Been doing some consulting with my brothers about the ranch," he said vaguely. "Security stuff."

"Well, you'd know about that. Better get a soda and get back to my seat. Second half's about to start. Nice to meet you, ma'am. Enjoy the game!"

Maybe he was back in Whiskey River more than usual, Brice thought. But he did need to keep poking around about the land sales—he'd found enough to fuel his suspicions and keep him going. And he did want to get to know Mary better—so he could make sure she was protected.

Of course, he liked her. And he was damn sure attracted to her. But he wasn't interested in getting involved, despite what Trey was hinting.

Well, he wouldn't mind being *involved*, as long as it was casual, nothing serious. He'd let his brothers do the marriage thing. He liked his freedom, not having anyone expecting him to be around every damn day like a lapdog, liked going where he liked, when he liked, without having to account to anyone for where he was and what he was doing. It was one of the things that had appealed to him about being a Ranger. Not being tied to one town, one area.

But looking down at Mary, who'd started talking with a just-returned Katie while he finished his chat with Trey, he was pretty sure she didn't do casual hookups. She was too private a person to let someone she knew only casually get that close to her.

The man who became her lover would have to earn the right. And be worthy of it.

Good thing he was mostly just interested in protecting her. Mostly. Then maybe, if they both wanted it, becoming closer friends.

After the second half started, he had her tell him what she saw in the plays. "It really is complex!" she said after a few series.

"Yes, that's what I like about football. All great sports require athletes to hone skills and learn strategy. Football just has so many more pieces that can fit together to make things work—or take them apart. The skill of the players, the timing of the plays—one second too soon or too late and you miss a handoff, or the receiver's not in the right spot to make a catch. The vast variety of plays that can be run on offense to move the ball, on defense to break up plays. Having to make snap decisions in seconds when something doesn't go right, how to recover and turn it, if possible, into an advantage. Or at least prevent disaster."

"Somebody needs to make a chart of that for real life," she said.

Something about the sudden bleakness on her face made him suspect she was recalling events in her own life that had ended in disaster. Was that why she'd come here, to free herself from the bonds of a past destroyed by trauma?

"It would be nice, wouldn't it? But there will never be a playbook for all of them. That's why the game's played by a team. You don't have to solve all the problems alone. Your teammates have your back, they watch out for you like you do for them, and you attack problems together." He looked into her eyes, hoping she understood he meant a lot more than football.

"Teamwork's a good thing, I guess."

"Usually. Sometimes it's hard to accept help. You want to do it all yourself. But it's almost always better to take that helping hand when it's offered."

"If it's offered by someone you can trust."

"Someone who's earned your trust," he confirmed.

Was he getting any closer to earning hers? Elaine had vouched for him and Bunny was his enthusiastic advocate, but Mary had to come to the conclusion that he was in fact trustworthy herself. Somehow, it had become really important to him that she did come to trust him. That she would be willing to put him on her team. As a friend. Maybe, eventually, as something more.

What else could he do to help her toward that belief?

Find and seize more opportunities to be with her. And hope, until she was ready to initiate meetings herself, that he continued to encounter her in town.

Another good reason to be around more often.

The game turned out to be a nail-biter, going down to the final minutes of the last quarter—where the opponent's linebacker managed to intercept Whiskey River's quarterback with the team backed up on their own twenty-yard line and run it in for the scoop and score, tying the game as time expired.

Mary, who'd jumped to her feet with the rest of the crowed, turned to him. "What happens now? The game ends in a tie?"

"No, it goes to overtime. There's another coin toss, the winner getting to choose to play offense or defense, the loser picking which side of the field the ball is placed on."

"Wouldn't the winner always want to play offense?" Mary asked.

"Usually they want to play defense. So they know how many points their offense will need to score to win."

"Okay. But what difference does it make what end of the field the ball is on? Doesn't seem like the loser gets to make a very useful choice."

"You pick the end of the field where most of your fans sit. So they will holler, stomp, clap, and generally make noise that distracts the opponent's offense and makes it harder for them to hear the play calls."

"Ah, I see. Strategy," she said with a nod.

"Always," Brice confirmed. "Looks like we won the toss, and yup, we're going to play defense first. You ready to holler?"

"As a loyal Whiskey River resident, it's my patriotic duty, right?"

Enjoying the sense of camaraderie, he said, "Absolutely."

The game went to three overtimes, the home team finally winning. Cheering, the brothers pounded each other on the back while the crowd hollered and whistled. "Phew, that one was way too close," Duncan said as they started walking out.

"I feel for the players on the opposing team," Mary said. "It must be tough to play your heart out for four quarters and three overtimes and then lose."

"It's never easy to lose when you've played your heart out, no matter what the score," Brice said.

Once again, sadness shadowed her eyes. "You're right about that."

When and where had she played her heart out and lost? More driven than ever, he felt driven to discover the cause of the melancholy he sensed behind her smile.

He walked with her group to the parking lot, trying to figure out how he might get to see her again, and not coming up with any smart ideas.

Then, as he halted beside her car to bid her good night, she said, "I was thinking . . . Elaine and Tom are going to a get-together tomorrow night with friends in town for homecoming. Bunny's going to come over to spend the night. Would you like to join us for dinner? You'd get a chance to use those cobalt-blue tumblers I bought at Old Man Tessel's. I wouldn't have found the place but for you, so I figure I owe you. Bunny would love to have you, I know."

His initial soar of delight abruptly nosedived. "I don't want it to be an *obligation.*" Then, taking a risk, he added, "I only want to join you if it would be a . . . pleasure. For you, as well as for Bunny."

Looking surprised by his comment and uncertain, she hesitated.

Way to go, stupid, he thought. *Should have just said "thank you" and accepted.* Then, while he waited for her to say "never mind, then," she said instead, "Okay. It would be a pleasure to have you join us for dinner."

He couldn't help the broad smile that sprang to his lips. "Never could refuse a lady who asks so nicely. What time would you like me to arrive?"

So exuberant, he almost didn't hear the time she mentioned, he exchanged a goodbye and headed back to his truck.

It was the first time she'd made an overture that neither he nor Bunny had maneuvered her into. Jettisoning the vague plans he'd made about joining Grant and Duncan at the town picnic without a qualm, he couldn't wait until Saturday night.

Chapter Seven

THE NEXT AFTERNOON, Mary kept telling herself not to be nervous. Brice McAllister had been to her house for dinner before.

Yes, except that time, Bunny forced you into it. This time you asked him of your own free will.

But she did owe him a favor. She was just being . . . neighborly.

Would he think she was encouraging him? Was she encouraging him?

Shoot, he was an attractive, interesting man. What was wrong with becoming friends? He hadn't signaled he wanted anything more than that.

Despite what her long-denied senses were whispering.

But that was a dead end, so no chance of going there.

Finally, she told herself to stop dithering. A darling little girl was coming over to help her simmer tomato sauce and make pasta noodles from scratch. Bunny would be delighted and fascinated by the entire process. She loved her uncle Brice and he loved her, so he'd be entirely content just to watch her enjoying it.

There wouldn't be any awkward moments alone with him.

It would be fine. He did make her laugh, after all, just like Bunny predicted. She should just relax and enjoy his company.

LATE THAT AFTERNOON, the tomato preparation assembly line ready, the ice crushed and in the freezer, the Parmesan shaved, and the pots and baking sheets ready, Mary walked over to get Bunny.

"Miss Mary!" the little girl cried, waving at her as soon as she walked into the Edgertons' backyard. "I'm so excited! Mommy, we're going to make tomato sauce and noodles and everything!"

"Honestly, I almost had to tie her to the back porch, she's been so eager to come over," Elaine said as Mary walked up the steps. "She would have gotten you out of bed this morning if I'd let her."

"That would have been fine," Mary said, giving the little girl a hug.

Then Brice walked out from the house, spiking a funny little leap in her heart that she told herself was nerves. "Hi, Brice."

"I was eager too. After our last dinner, I can't wait to taste your homemade tomato sauce and pasta."

"We'd better get it started. To make my *nonna's* recipe, we should simmer the tomatoes for a whole day, but we'll make do with several hours. You and Tom have a great time tonight and don't worry, Elaine. I'll take good care of Bunny." Turning back to the child, she said, "We'll have a great dinner with Uncle Brice and after he leaves, we'll get in our jammies and have a girls' night in."

"With stories and everything?"

"Stories and everything."

"And applesauce pancakes in the morning?"

"Applesauce pancakes and bacon."

"Shoot, I may have to invite myself back for breakfast," Brice said.

"Y'all have fun, and remember, you can call me anytime," Elaine said. "Text me some pictures of Bunny making spaghetti noodles, please!"

"Will do. Bye, Elaine."

"See you tomorrow, Mommy," Bunny said, giving her mother a hug and big kiss. "Ready, Miss Mary?"

"So soon they abandon you," Elaine said, with a mock sigh.

"For homemade pasta and tomato sauce?" Brice said. "That just about does trump 'Mommy.'"

"Hush, now," Mary said. "Nothing trumps Mommy. But even Mommy can lend her princess to a best friend for the night."

"Right. And you're my bestest friend. You and Uncle

Brice!" Bunny said, linking arms with each of them as they gave her mom a final wave goodbye and walked across the lawn to the gate leading into Mary's garden.

"There are bowls on the back porch. We have to pick tomatoes, basil, and oregano so we can start the sauce. Then, when it's almost done simmering, we'll make the noodles."

As Bunny ran toward the porch, Mary turned to Brice. "There's a bowl for you too. Tomato sauce takes a lot of tomatoes. It's labor intensive, so I always make about eight pints of sauce at once."

"That's a lot of spaghetti!"

"I use the sauce for all sorts of things—meatballs, lasagna, chicken cacciatore, salsa, to name just a few. If I want to be really industrious, I'll can some, since the canned jars keep longer, but the spaghetti sauce for tonight will take a pint or more, and what we make today will stay tasty in the freezer for three months. I'll easily use it up before then, so I usually skip the extra time needed to can. Did your mom not can food when you were growing up on the ranch?"

"My stepmom wasn't much for extra kitchen work, and we boys were busy enough on the ranch without a big garden to tend. Sure, we grew black-eyed peas and tomatoes and peppers and sometimes squash, though usually the squash bugs got that just about the time it started producing something edible. But we grew just enough for us to eat fresh." He smiled. "Even then, we complained about having to weed the patch."

Picking up bowls from the porch, she walked over with him to the tomato section of the garden, where Bunny was waiting, her own bowl in hand. "Pick some of those oblong-shaped ones," Mary said, pointing to the plant. "Only ones that are nice and red. Then some of the big ones here."

"You've got a pretty large garden—I hadn't noticed just how large last time. Must keep you busy weeding."

"I don't mind," she said as she picked tomatoes and put them in the bowl. "I find it relaxing. And satisfying, seeing all the plants growing together in harmony. The sweet scents of the flowers, the sharp tang of herbs, the vegetative odor of grass and tomatoes and green peppers surrounding you while you work. I love it."

"I like flowers with vegetables," Bunny announced. "These are pretty colors, but they smell bad."

"Marigolds," Mary said. "Bugs think they smell bad, too, so they help protect the tomatoes. But the roses are pretty, and these smell good. The tomatoes protect them."

Brice raised his eyebrows. "Do they?"

"Garden lore says they do, though there isn't a lot of scientific research to back it up. But not everything has to be verified in a laboratory. Observation, experience, and intuition count too."

"They sure do in my job."

Mary frowned a little. She preferred not to remember what his job was. When he was in Whiskey River, he was off duty and never in uniform, which made it easier to forget. If she was going to enjoy his company, it was better that way.

Shaking off that momentary irritation, she said, "Besides, flowers make the garden pretty, whether they actually help protect the plants or not. How many tomatoes do you have, Bunny?"

"Six."

"Okay, we'll need about thirty. Let's finish picking them and then we'll get some basil and oregano."

"And some roses, too? So the house will smell good?"

"Roses, too, if you want some. You'll need your garden gloves, though, so the thorns don't get you."

"My bowl's full," Bunny said, handing it to Mary. "Can I get the snippers for the roses now?"

"Sure. Don't forget your gloves."

As Bunny ran off, Mary smiled. "She's so energetic and enthusiastic. So sure the world is a wonderful place, each day a new present to be unwrapped."

"Children should grow up feeling that way. Loved, wanted, protected, sure the world belongs to them."

She sighed as a flash of memory of herself at Bunny's age zipped into her head. Uncle Sal tossing her into the air to her squeals of delight. How she'd loved his attention . . . once. "Yes, they should enjoy that fantasy. All too soon they grow old enough to discover the world is often not at all what it seems."

Enjoy it before knowledge stripped away those childhood illusions to reveal the bitter truth.

"Ah, the trick is to accept the reality of the world but not let it kill your dreams or your optimism," Brice said.

She swallowed hard, remembering her engagement party—she and Ian, holding hands, smiling. Before the world changed forever. "Sometimes that's hard to do," she said softly, looking away.

He tipped her chin up to face him. "That's why you have a team of friends to help."

A team to help. Is that what he wanted to do? Be added to the small team who supported her in Whiskey River—Elaine and Tom and Shirley?

Did she want to add him?

Pushing away that question for which she didn't yet have a firm answer, she nodded. "And delights like Bunny to remind you of what the world might be like. Even if it is a fast-fading fantasy."

"Then you make it last as long as possible."

She turned away from the sympathy in his eyes that inexplicably brought tears to her own. It was foolish to think he was empathizing with her for what had happened in the past, since she'd revealed nothing. And had no plans to. At least . . . not yet.

"I think we have enough tomatoes now."

He followed her to the porch, put down the colanders heavy with fruit, and went to help Bunny cut some fragrant Cinco de Mayo floribunda roses, their swirls of vivid coral-pink petals and gold stamens as attractive as the strong, old-rose scent. Then they plucked some rosemary sprigs to add to the display.

Shedding their muddy shoes at the door, they padded into the kitchen and scrubbed the garden dirt off their hands.

"We use boiling water to get the tomatoes ready, so I don't want you next to the stove," she told Bunny as she got out a vase for her flowers. "I'll boil them for half a minute, then put them in an ice-water bath. Your job is to spoon them out of the ice water and put them on a tray for me. But if you get tired, you can work on the new puzzle I got you."

"I won't get tired. I'm making tomato sauce for dinner!"

"Okay, ready to get started?" she asked, turning on the heat under the sauce pot.

"Ready!" Bunny called, jumping up and down.

"As soon as the water is simmering, we can start. We'll cook the tomatoes in the hot water and cool them in your cold water. Once they are all done, we'll peel off the skin and you can put them in the food processor and chop them."

"I can peel the tomatoes as you go," Brice offered.

"Are you sure?"

"I may not be a gourmet cook, but I think I can handle that. It would make the process go faster, wouldn't it?"

He did like to be helpful. Appreciative of that, she said, "Yes, it would. There's a compost bucket by the sink—you can put the skins in that."

With her three-person team set up, the work went much

more quickly than when she did it alone. Bunny was delighted to play "fish the tomato out of the water" while Brice quickly sloughed off the peels and dropped the skinned tomatoes into the bowl. In record time, they were ready for Bunny to spoon the naked tomatoes into the food processor, then press the button to chop them, after which Brice dumped the processor bowl into the sauce pot, where the chopped tomatoes began to simmer.

"We'll add the spices at the end, but for now, we'll just let it cook."

"Can I make noodles now?"

"We won't need them until the sauce is almost done. How about we make something we can eat right away? You love cheese, right?"

"Yum," Bunny confirmed. Mary looked over to Brice, who nodded.

"How about we make bird nests?"

"Bird nests?" Bunny frowned. "Eat twigs and moss and stuff? Yuck!"

"No, silly," Mary laughed, ruffling Bunny's hair. "We'll make the nests out of this." She walked to the fridge and took out the bowl of shaved Parmesan cheese, then brought it over to the worktable along with a large spoon.

"Spoon the cheese into little nests on the baking sheet—about one large spoonful per nest, with about two inches between them," she told Brice. "Then we'll bake them in the oven and in ten minutes, cheese snacks!"

Brice helped Bunny put the cheese onto the baking sheet the correct distance apart. After Mary put the trays into the oven, the smell of toasting cheese mingled with the odors of fresh-cooked tomatoes.

"Good thing we're making something to eat. It already smells so good, I'm starving," Brice announced.

"We have time before we need to start on the noodles. Who wants to play a game?"

"Me!" Bunny cried.

"Get out your favorite one, and I'll get us a drink. Milk or lemonade?"

"Milk," Bunny said.

"Water?" she asked Brice.

"Please. I'm hoping for wine with the spaghetti later."

"Always."

"I'm astounded you managed to cook as much as you have thus far without any wine in your hand."

"Don't worry," she said, enjoying his lighthearted teasing. "It'll be five o'clock soon."

THE NEXT FEW hours passed companionably, washing up the prep tools she would need again later, playing games with Bunny while munching on the crunchy Parmesan nests, occasionally stirring the simmering sauce, taking a walk into the garden to pick more roses, as well as vegetables to make their salad.

While she washed the arugula and tossed it with store-bought romaine, salad greens not being amendable to growing in the heat of Texas in the early fall, Brice cut up the vegetables, fashioning the tomatoes into odd shapes and asking Bunny to guess what they were. As he had with her at the flea market, the identities he proposed—vampire, boulder, dog, horse, were so outlandishly unlike the shapes he'd made that he kept them both laughing.

Watching him with Bunny, Mary felt something twist in her heart. He might be a lawman, a type she instinctively mistrusted, but there was something enormously appealing about a man who delighted in spending so much time entertaining a six-year-old. His patience with her, his encouragement, and the sheer joy she saw in his face as he made Bunny laugh filled her with admiration and a bittersweet melancholy.

Ian would have been like that with our children, she thought sadly. Would she ever get over that loss?

Then she chided herself, as she did whenever melancholy took hold. She'd survived, she had a job working with books she loved, a wonderful house, a great garden, and a kind neighbor who frequently let her borrow her precious daughter. She could walk down a street without having to look behind her, make her plans and go about her business without worrying that someone was scheming to make Uncle Sal's little princess either a reward or a target. Papa had broken away, too, and was safe in Florida, making a new life with a new love.

With so many blessings, it was as ungrateful as it was futile to pine for what might have been, she told herself as she checked the sauce. As Papa always said, make the best of what you have, and it will always be enough.

Determining the sauce had simmered to perfection, she added herbs and got out the flour, olive oil, sea salt and eggs.

"Time to make the noodles," she announced, taking the clean processor from the dishwasher and putting it on the worktable beside Bunny. After quickly blending the flour, oil and egg mixture, she let Bunny help spread it out with the rolling pin before putting it into the attachment on her food processor. After cutting and rolling, cutting and rolling, she let Bunny feed the flattened dough layers into the pasta-cutter. She chuckled as the little girl whooped with glee when the flat rectangles separated into long, noodly strands and smiled as Brice took photos to text to Bunny's parents.

"We make this last because the fresh noodles only need to cook for a minute before they're ready to eat," she told Brice.

"Thank heaven," he said, groaning. "Smelling all that good food makes me so hungry I'm about to expire."

"Help Bunny set the table," she said tartly. "It'll take your mind off your imminent demise."

"Let's light candles too," Bunny said, after the cutlery and dishes were in place. "Mommy says we always have candles with a special dinner. This one's really special 'cause I helped make all of it myself!"

"You did, and we can't wait to taste it," Brice said. "Let's fix plates, then we'll take another pic to text to your mommy and daddy."

With the picture taken, the table set, the candles lit, the wine poured, and the plates arranged with noodles topped with steaming sauce and a grating of fresh Parmesan, Mary felt light . . . as if a bubble of happiness had lifted her above her workaday cares and sad memories. It was maybe the most content she'd felt since arriving in Whiskey River.

She was inordinately pleased when, after his first bite, Brice looked over, his eyes wide. "This is fantastic! So much better than dry, store-bought pasta, it can't even compare."

"Thank you, kind sir."

"You're welcome, Uncle Brice," Bunny chimed in.

"I may have to commission you two to make fresh pasta for me once a week."

"Yeah! Then you'd have to come to Whiskey River once a week to get it," Bunny said.

"Are you not always here once a week?" Mary asked, surprised. She knew she'd seen him at least that often.

He looked a little uncomfortable, which was odd. "Not until I started looking into . . . things on the ranch."

"Is that progressing?"

"Not yet. I'll keep plugging away. Something will develop."

"Just make sure you don't reshape the facts to fit your theory," she said with some asperity.

He looked up, surprised and a bit indignant. "I should resent that remark. I'll have you know I always, *always* let the facts shape my theory."

Did he? She really didn't know how he operated. Maybe he was different from the cops she'd known. Maybe he didn't take his foregone conclusions and try to shoehorn people to fit into them.

In any event, she'd offended him. Pouring him a glass of wine, she said, "Sorry, I didn't mean to insult you. Am I forgiven?"

To her relief, he smiled. "A lady who cooks like you do and pours great wine is forgiven anything."

After dinner, Mary took Bunny to change into her jammies and then adjourned to the couch to have ice cream for dessert. The little girl soon faded, dozing off in the corner, hugging her stuffed bear. Nodding in her direction, Brice said, "Should I carry her off to bed?"

"Yes. I don't think she's going to revive."

"It was a big day. She made her first Italian dinner from scratch."

"She did a great job too."

"Just as great as her teacher." He gave her an admiring glance. "If you decide to open your own restaurant, let me know. I'll be a backer—and a customer."

"I enjoy cooking when I feel like it and there's no timeline. There'd be too frantic a pace, running a restaurant. It would take the joy out of it." She walked with him as he carried the little girl to the bed in the guest room and turned down the covers. He tucked Bunny in, brushing a lock of hair from her face, then kissed her on the forehead. "She sure is a darling."

"That she is," Mary whispered, holding back the tears, brought back once again to the moment the doctors had told her she'd lost her baby. That it was unlikely she'd ever have another. *You have this time with Bunny. It will be enough. You'll make it enough.*

When they walked back out to the living room, Brice remained standing, not returning to the couch but not heading for the door. Lingering.

She found to her surprise she wasn't ready for him to leave yet, either. "How about some coffee with a dash of amaretto before you go?"

"I'd like that. I do feel a little guilty. We took so long over dinner, I cheated your number one fan out of the 'girls' evening' you promised."

"That's okay. We'll have a 'girls' morning' to make up for it."

"Then I'd love that coffee. It'll keep me awake for the drive back up to the ranch."

"I thought you didn't want to stay with your newlywed brothers."

"I'm not. I'm staying at the house Harrison's dad built

on the part of the ranch he bought."

"The one that's being converted to an event center?"

"Yes. Since I'm back and forth more often, looking into things, my brothers didn't want me paying to stay at the B&B."

"How is the renovation going?" she asked as she set about making espresso.

"Grant's done about as much as he can. Now they're just waiting for the small business loan to come through to fund adding bathrooms and bedrooms in the barn. They hope to have it open in time to host Christmas events. Grant is excited about giving kids on the military bases in the city a chance to experience ranch life."

"It would be a real gift. It's so beautiful here."

"Everything you hoped for when you took the job?"

"Everything and more."

"I hope good friends are part of that 'more.'" He took a sip of coffee, then paused as if deciding whether or not to say anything else.

"What is it?"

"It might be too soon to tell you this, but . . . I'd ask you out, if I didn't think you'd turn me down. I don't want to pry and I sure don't want to be threatening. But . . . I like you, Mary. A lot."

An eddy of warmth and attraction filled her. "I like you too."

"I'm glad. But don't worry. I'm a patient guy. We can

take this as slowly as you want."

She felt tears sting her eyes. "I appreciate that. I . . . I don't know where I want this to go. It's been so long . . . that part of me . . . seemed to have died."

"You lost someone." A statement, not a question.

Nodding, she wiped away a tear.

"You don't want to talk about it."

Not trusting herself to speak, she shook her head.

He smiled. "Dang, girl, most women I've known can't wait to talk about *everything*, including a lot I'd rather not hear. But I'm still a good listener, if and when you ever do want to talk."

"Okay. I'll remember that." After a moment of panic when she feared he'd start to press her, she felt a rush of relief. He was understanding—not threatening. He wouldn't push her further than she was ready to go.

He drained the rest of his coffee. "Before I leave, I think you need one new Texas expression."

"Since your job as a native Texas is to educate me," she said, amused.

"That's right. After that fabulous meal, 'if I felt any better, I'd drop my harp plumb through a cloud.'"

She laughed. "I must admit, I'm feeling pretty good too."

"I'm glad." He looked for a moment like he might say more, but didn't.

Once again, she was relieved he was so forbearing, not asking questions she wasn't ready to answer or pushing for something she wasn't yet ready to give. Even though she felt a little guilty; he'd been so open about his own life, and she'd not reciprocated at all.

But not guilty enough to divulge what she wasn't ready to talk about.

"I better hit the road. You'll be up early with a little girl eager for pancakes and bacon." He walked with her to the door. "Thanks again for a wonderful evening."

She laughed. "You must be one of the few single men who could say that about sharing the evening with a six-year-old."

"I've always loved kids. Who could resist Bunny?"

"No sane person. Good night, Brice. And . . . I had a wonderful evening too."

The smile that lit his face sent little ripples of delight, attraction—and alarm—through her. "Good. Hope to see you soon."

She watched him walk out to his truck under a night sky spangled with stars, just a hint of coolness in the air hinting of fall to come. His stride was confident, purposeful, a man at ease in his own skin, content with himself. Large, commanding, but not dominating or threatening. A big man who could sit on the floor playing card games with a little girl.

Yes, she thought she might enjoy seeing more of Brice McAllister. As long as he was content not to take things too far, too fast.

And if she could ever get beyond the knowledge that he was a cop.

Chapter Eight

TEN DAYS LATER, Brice left Austin after finishing a week of intensive refresher training with his SWAT team. He usually enjoyed the break from his normal routine, the chance to hone skills and learn the latest changes in tactics and restrictions—always changing restrictions. This time, he'd been impatient for the training to end so he could get back to his official investigation into a case of bank fraud—especially since tracking down potential suspicious deposits in small community banks meant he could base his operations out of the Scott ranch house in Whiskey River, rather than his condo in Austin.

It meant he got to see his brothers and his friends more often.

Friends like Bunny, whom he promised during the spaghetti dinner at Mary's to take exploring around the ranch the next time he returned to Whiskey River—so, hopefully, he could persuade her lovely neighbor to come along.

Slow at it was, he was making progress with Mary. She hadn't retreated completely when he'd mentioned dating . . . eventually. He had teased out the fact that she'd lost someone, probably a boyfriend or maybe a husband, and wasn't over that loss yet. Which might explain why she never talked about her past or her family.

If that was the reason for her reticence, it might mean she hadn't run from some form of abuse, but had needed to start over again in a place that didn't remind her of what she'd lost.

He told her he'd be patient, and he intended to be. Initially, he'd wanted to get closer so he could figure out whether she was under some sort of threat. He still did, though with her seeming more mournful than scared, that now seemed less likely. But now . . . he wanted more.

He wanted to get closer because he found the time he spent with her so fulfilling.

He'd always enjoyed being around his family and he loved kids. Time spent that Saturday afternoon and evening, just doing simple things, like picking produce from the garden, cooking, and playing games with Bunny, had created within him a warm, expansive contentment. He'd given Mary the quote about dropping his harp because it was so apt—so apt it shocked him into realizing that he could envision, even anticipate, having a future like this. A wife like Mary to cook and garden with and tease, to sit with over a candlelit dinner table sharing wine and conversation. Playing with, raising, and cherishing a child, like Bunny.

Though he shouldn't have been too shocked. Much as he liked his independence, by the time he met Ashley, living the idle single lifestyle had already started to pale. He'd begun to envision the possibility of settling down with one special woman, although he'd still pictured living that life in the city. After dating Ashley on and off for about a year, he'd believed it when she claimed to love him and promised she wanted only him—until she'd inadvertently texted him a message to "her darling Kurt," arranging to meet the man at a hotel for the weekend during a time when Brice was going to be out of Austin on a case.

Thank heavens he hadn't yet made her the proposal he'd been contemplating.

Her betrayal had soured him on dating for sure, but even once he got over the hurt and anger—fortunately, he'd never gotten to the point of believing himself completely in love with her—he found he just didn't have the enthusiasm he used to have to go back to hooking up at a bar with a hot babe interested in a short, sex-fueled relationship.

Maybe it was his brothers' obvious happiness in their new lives as married men that had him thinking about long term again, or how much he appreciated the witty, smart, creative women they'd married. Women with whom, as the day at Abby's shop and the night at the football game demonstrated, Mary fit in perfectly. She was already besties with Abby and Katie.

Maybe it was just the sexy, complex puzzle that was Mary Williams, who captivated him more than any woman he'd encountered before—even Ashley.

She certainly attracted him, which was both a plus and a problem.

Sitting beside her on the couch, supremely aware of her lovely body and luscious lips so close, he probably could have used a dowsing in that ice-water bath they'd used for the tomatoes. He was a simple male, not always as sensitive to female signals as he'd like, but he knew without a doubt that if she was not yet ready to talk to him about what she'd lost, she was definitely not ready for kissing.

No matter how much he ached to hold her, breathe in her rose perfume, and kiss those tempting lips.

All he knew was he was eager to see her again, glad the requirements of his job and on-again, off-again investigation into the harassment against the Triple A allowed him to return to Whiskey River.

Maybe one day soon he'd win both her confidence—and that kiss.

But . . . he couldn't help noticing, unlike almost everyone else he'd met who, when they found out he was a Texas Ranger, expressed admiration and awe, Mary never asked him anything about the job. Quite the opposite; she seemed to grow chilly or even . . . hostile whenever he alluded to it. What was it she'd said? *Just make sure you don't reshape the facts to fit your theory* of who might be responsible for the actions against the Triple A?

He suspected she'd had some sort of unpleasant run-in with the law. Or, if not personally, then someone close to her had. She sure didn't look at lawmen as protectors and seemed to struggle to accept that aspect of who he was.

As he grew to like her more and more, he was glad he wasn't usually uniformed when he saw her. He suspected that if he were still a regular cop wearing police blue, it would have snuffed out anything between them before it could begin.

But why?

Pressing her for the reason wouldn't help—what was it she had said? *I'm . . . very private myself, so if I see someone pestering people with questions, I tend to feel that they are being . . . harassed.*

He'd just have to add that question to the other mysteries about her he wanted to solve.

He would go slow and steady, just like he'd promised. But eventually, he vowed to himself, he would convince her it was safe for her to tell him everything.

After checking out some bank branches in San Marcos and Blanco today, he'd stop by Elaine and Tom's to set a time for that weekend excursion with Bunny before heading back to the ranch. Who, if she didn't suggest it before he did, probably would be delighted to add her next-door, "bestest" friend to their outing.

IN THE LATE afternoon, Brice pulled up in front of Elaine

and Tom's Victorian. His knock at the door brought Tom, who welcomed him with a one-armed guy hug. "I know, you came to set a time for Bunny's ranch trip. Can you linger for a while? We're having a little happy hour on the back porch—with Bunny's favorite neighbor," Tom added, wagging his eyebrows suggestively.

Despite the immediate spike in his pulse, Brice tried to act nonchalant. "Yes, I have time."

"You seem to be getting along really well with Miss Mary—according to Bunny," Tom probed.

"How hard is it to get along with a woman who loves kids, cooks like a master chef, and looks like a model?"

"Point taken. You . . . developing an interest there?"

"I agreed with Elaine that there might be something threatening in her past. The only way to find out for sure if there is some danger somewhere is to get to know her better. But I have to take it very easy. Because she's still wary."

"If she's still resisting you, there must really be something going on. Normally women go after you faster than a prairie fire with a tailwind. What can I fix you?"

"Better make mine soda water with a twist. I have to drive up to the ranch afterward."

"Boring, but responsible. But then, you are a Texas Ranger."

Brice walked out toward the back porch, where he could see Elaine laughing as Bunny sat on Mary's lap while they played a bouncing game. Brice halted, just watching, thinking what an appealing picture they made—the laughing, exuberant little girl and the dark-haired beauty whose concentration was focused solely on the child.

Bunny looked up first and spied him. "Uncle Brice!" she cried, hopping off Mary's lap to run over and give him a hug. "I'm so glad you're back!"

"I'm glad to be back, too, peanut."

"I see you survived your SWAT refresher," Elaine said, motioning him to a seat on the bench beside her. "I don't even see any cuts and bruises."

"The worst ones are hidden," he deadpanned.

"Brice isn't just a Ranger, he's a sharpshooter," Tom said as he joined them. "Gets called out whenever there's a hostage situation or an active-shooter incident."

"Fortunately, that doesn't happen too often," Brice said, watching Mary's face to see if the comments would arouse the subtle negative response any mention of police work usually elicited.

But she seemed to be wholly concentrated on Bunny, who'd hopped back onto her lap for more bouncing games.

"In between times, we don't know what he does," Tom said.

"Very hush-hush," Elaine teased.

"If you're finished abusing me, let me have some of those snacks."

"We made cheese nests, Uncle Brice," Bunny said.

He took one, winking at Mary as he took a bite. "Delicious. I wish you were close enough to Austin to make me cheese nests every time I came home from work."

"Why don't you just stay here?" Bunny said. "You could come over to Miss Mary's every day and we'd make cheese nests for you."

"Bunny, you can't volunteer someone else's house and time," Elaine reproved.

"She's also volunteering her own, and that's very generous," Mary said.

"I appreciate it," Brice said. "And I may take you up on it more often. So what's it to be at the ranch, Bunny? Rock collecting? Visiting the cows?"

"Riding Moondust!" she cried. "While we visit cows and collect some rocks." Her eyes lit with sudden interest. "Miss Mary, can you come too? We can find some pretty rocks for your garden."

Silently thanking Bunny, Brice said, "Please do come along, if you can spare the time. The Triple A offers a great selection of rocks for your garden. Besides, I'd like to show you around the ranch. Show you the legacy we're preserving. Grant will be mowing, but we could probably meet Abby at the cabin on her lunch break, and she could show you through. Abby could bring Katie along to play with Bunny. I can grab us something for lunch, so Abby doesn't feel like she has to feed us."

"You should go see the cabin," Elaine recommended. "Abby's renovation is amazing! We got to see it when she and Grant got married—they held the wedding there."

"The Triple A is a beautiful spread," Tom added.

Having tossed in Abby and Katie as extra incentives, Brice held his breath, knowing Bunny was sure to add more persuasion if needed.

But instead, Mary shrugged. "With so many stellar recommendations, how could I not go see it?"

"A ride, collecting rocks, a picnic on the heights—how could you resist?" Brice teased.

"I would like to see the ranch and the cabin. Abby's told me so much about it. But . . . I don't know how to ride."

"We have a nice, easy mare for you. I can even lead her if you like. Traveling by horseback is the best way to see the ranch, since not all parts of it are accessible by road and some of the roads we do have are pretty rough. I'd rather not take my truck on them if I don't have to."

She paused, looking uncertain. "You're sure the mare would be suitable for someone who's never ridden?"

"Like sitting in a rocking chair, I promise."

"You'll love it, Miss Mary! I get to ride Katie's pony, Moondust, and it's so much fun. We can take buckets to collect rocks and we'll see pretty birds and lots of cows. Miss Harrison's special cows even have names! But Uncle Brice won't let me pet them. You'll come, won't you?"

"How could I pass up meeting cows who have names?" she said with a smile.

"The named animals are my sister-in-law's herd bulls,"

Brice said. "Her late father was a top breeder. A retired Navy man, he named the bulls after famous sea captains. Halsey, Nimitz."

"I really have to see them now. Although I have no idea what a 'herd bull' is. I'm afraid I know almost nothing about ranching."

"Don't worry, Brice will give you the short version," Tom said. "Better not ask Duncan—ranching's in his blood, and he's so enthused, he thinks everyone should be. He's likely to give you an hour's lecture if you give him the least encouragement."

"Great!" Brice said. "I'll set it up with Abby to visit the cabin. We'll have our picnic on the deck there, overlooking the hills and the creek. I'll have sunscreen and bug spray, but bring your own if you require anything special."

She nodded. "Bug spray. Anything biting loves me."

Brice bit his lip to keep from adding he could understand that. He'd love a taste of her himself.

"I'll pick you and Bunny up here before lunch Saturday, then."

"Yeah!" Bunny said, giving Mary a hug and then coming over to hug Brice. "Riding, and rocks, and a picnic. And I get to play with Katie!"

"It's settled then," Brice said, setting down his empty glass, delighted with how things had turned out. He'd been smart to count on Bunny. "Thanks for the drink, Tom. I'd better head out. I texted Harrison that I'd arrive in time for dinner."

"If you'll be doing the touring, donating the rocks, and making sure I don't kill myself my first time on a horse, I can at least bring the picnic lunch," Mary said. "Tell Abby I'll fix enough for all of us."

"I'm certainly not going to pass that offer up."

"If it's okay with your mommy, you can come over Saturday morning and help me put together the lunch," Mary said to Bunny. "We'll make enough to leave some for your mommy and daddy too."

"Can I, Mommy?"

"Of course," Tom answered for her. "A man would have to be a certified fool to pass up a chance to eat Mary's cooking. Not that my darling wife is any slouch in the meal-preparation department."

"Good save," Elaine said, giving her husband a speaking glance. "Sure, honey, you can help Miss Mary make lunch for us."

"Thanks again for the offer," Brice said. "See you all Saturday, then."

Bunny grabbed his hand and walked him out to his truck.

"Thanks, Uncle Brice. It's going to be so much fun! I can't wait."

Since she'd been responsible, as he'd hoped, for persuading Mary to accompany them, he was much more thankful to her. "You're very welcome, peanut."

After giving her a toss in the air, making her shriek with delight, he sent her back to the house and drove off.

A whole day with Mary, showing her the places he loved. Yeah, he couldn't wait either.

BRICE WOKE UP early Saturday morning with the sense that it was going to be a special day. He grinned when he remembered why. He was going to be able to spend time with two of his favorite people.

Padding out of the bedroom barefoot, he made coffee, then took a cup out on the north terrace and watched the sun rising pink and golden in the eastern sky.

He appreciated the loan of the Scott ranch house. A comfortable, sprawling place, it was surrounded by porches on three sides that offered great views, especially the north porch off the kitchen and family room. The covered area overlooked a meadow that curved gently down to the banks of the creek that wound its way around the eastern side of the Triple A. Grant and Abby's renovated cabin was located even farther east, not far from the boundary line of the ranch.

If they'd made the tour in the spring, Brice could have shown Mary meadows of bluebonnets. There wasn't much blooming now after the heat of the summer, but fall asters were winking their starry violet blossoms and the gayflowers' spikes of purple still decorated the rocky landscape. He'd be proud to show off the land that had been in his family for generations.

Once upon a time, he'd thought to sell out his share to Duncan, maybe settle permanently in Austin. He had enjoyed, he admitted, his first few years in the city. The nightlife, the friendly ladies, the music and film scene. But lately, he was finding the traffic and busyness annoying, finding himself yearning for the wide-open spaces and serenity of the ranch. After his unpleasant breakup with Ashley, he felt even more renewed and refreshed living out here in the pure, honest air.

He hadn't spent this much time at the ranch in years, probably not since before he left for college. His roots in this Hill Country soil must go deeper than he'd thought, for he was starting to consider selling his downtown condo and buying a smaller place to use as a pied-à-terre when he needed to stay in the city. He was glad now that Duncan had resisted when he'd casually mentioned selling, saying their father wanted all of them to remain owners, even though Duncan would be the one to run the ranch.

Maybe he'd build a house somewhere on the property and use that as his base instead of Austin. Or maybe buy a cottage in town, like the one Mary was renting.

Maybe eventually share a home with her.

That thought crept in before he was aware of it. Not too long ago, such an idea would have surprised him, but this time, he only thought it . . . curious. He was definitely interested in spending more time with her. But he wasn't close to being sure that meant forever.

He finished his coffee and went back inside to refresh it and throw together some cereal to eat while he checked email to see if any of his team had turned up other evidence in the bank fraud case they were working. Whoever was doing the bank transfers was clever and had avoided leaving a trail so far. The originator of the bank-to-bank transfers was hard to trace, especially if the one doing it was on the inside and knew all the necessary codes. But Brice knew if they kept at it, eventually, they'd pin the perpetrator down. The individual would get greedy, make a mistake, leave a tell. They almost always did.

A few hours later, shaved and showered, Brice donned a clean shirt, tromping jeans, and sturdy boots, and walked out to his truck, his heart rate already rising in anticipation. If his luck held, today he'd show Mary the beauty of the Triple A.

After a pleasant drive through the late-morning sunshine into town, he pulled up in front of Elaine and Tom's big Victorian. Bunny must have been watching, for she ran out to meet him before he even got out of the truck.

"I got my bug spray and a container for rocks. And Mommy gave me an apple to feed Moondust. Let's get Miss Mary and go!"

Wait until he broke it to her about the change in plans, Brice thought regretfully. She was going to be so disappointed. Hopefully, the change wouldn't send Mary running too.

"Whoa, peanut, let me at least say 'hi' to your folks first," Brice said, picking the girl up and hoisting her onto his shoulders. "It's not polite for me to just rush off with you."

He walked in and greeted her parents, who were having coffee with Mary. Brice's heart did a little flip the minute he saw her, and he knew he was smiling. She looked lovely, the ugly sack dress exchanged for a slim pair of jeans, some sturdy walking shoes, and a sleeveless blouse in a golden hue that complemented her eyes. All she needed were some proper boots and a Stetson, and she'd look like a real Texas woman.

"Ready to go?" Bunny said, running over to tug Mary's hand. "A picnic and riding Moondust and collecting rocks! It'll be *perfect*!"

"It's always perfect when you spend time with your favorite people," Brice said. "But we're going to have to change the activities a little. We'll still go out to the cabin, but my brother called me this morning and said Moondust has a sore foot. Must have picked up a rock in her shoe somewhere. He said you wouldn't be able to ride her today."

Bunny's smile crumpled. "I can't ride Moondust?"

"Sorry, peanut. But how about this? After we meet Miss Abby at the cabin and have our picnic, she said you could come back with her and play with Katie and her cousin, Sissie. You know how much fun they are."

"Play with Katie and Sissie?" Bunny echoed, looking a

bit brighter.

"Yes, if that's okay with your parents." After Elaine gave him a nod, he said, "We'll still have our picnic, and I'll arrange another ride for you as soon as Moondust is better. Deal?" He held out his hand.

After a disappointed sigh, Bunny shook his hand. "Deal."

"So we'll come back after the picnic?" Mary asked.

"Not unless you want to. Bunny's already seen the ranch, but I'd still like to show you around the Triple A. Are we still on for that?"

While he held his breath, Mary paused, obviously considering. Then nodded. "Yes, I would like to see the ranch."

"Great! You guys going out this afternoon?" he asked Elaine and Tom.

"Thought we'd walk downtown after we eat Mary's luscious salad, maybe have a coffee at Reba's."

"Kinda like a date?" Brice asked.

"Kinda," Elaine said with a wicked little smile. "We might even do a little lingerie shopping at the Fallen Angels boutique."

Brice put his hands over Bunny's ears. "Better get this poor innocent girl out of here before she hears something she shouldn't. Let me carry the picnic basket, ma'am," he offered, following Mary to the table where she'd gone to retrieve a large basket.

"I can handle it," Mary said.

"I know you can, but you made the lunch. I can at least tote it."

"Let him. Makes him feel all masculine and commanding to be useful," Tom said with a grin, walking out with them. "Have fun, sweetheart," he added, giving his daughter a hug.

"Abby will drop Bunny off when she brings Sissie back to town," Brice said. "She'll have her back before dark."

"That will be perfect," Elaine said. "Have a great day, all of you!"

The three of them walked to the truck. Brice hopped Bunny into the back and buckled her into the car seat he kept there just for her, then turned to help Mary up the high step into the passenger seat. The jolt of sensation he felt when he took her hand made him freeze, even as her eyes widened. For a moment, the two of them just stood there, looking at each other. Her gaze was startled—but he read attraction in it too.

What would it be like if she were to go up on tiptoe and kiss him?

Like heaven, probably, he answered himself. But no sense getting all heated up. He hadn't even learned her story yet, and something told him she'd have to be comfortable enough to tell him about who she was before she'd be anywhere near ready to kiss him.

Still, he felt encouraged by that electric connection—and the knowledge that she'd not only felt it, too, but she hadn't jerked her hand free or retreated.

"Can we go now, Uncle Brice?" Bunny's voice recalled them.

"Sure, peanut. Let Miss Mary get her seat belt fastened and we'll be off." With the hand he still held, he gave her a boost up.

"Abby texted that she'd meet us at the cabin just after noon," he told Mary as they headed out of town.

"I'm looking forward to seeing it."

"You won't be disappointed. It's a showpiece."

Mary was quiet on the drive, Bunny more than making up for her spot in the conversation. Something Brice had noticed when they had dinner at her place. She encouraged Bunny to talk, encouraged him to talk, but didn't talk a lot herself. It certainly wasn't because she was dull or inarticulate. She just had a sort of quiet self-confidence that didn't require her to be the center of attention. He liked that.

Half an hour later, he turned off the country road onto a long drive, passing beneath a metal archway with a hanging sign announcing "Triple A." "From here on, we'll be on McAllister land," he told Mary.

"Why was the ranch named the Triple A?" she asked.

"My great-great-grandfather, Alastair, settled here in the 1870s with his wife, Alice, and son, Archibald."

"Did he come from another part of the states?"

"No, directly from Scotland. He'd raised cattle there and heard there was open land to be had in the Texas territory, so he packed up his wife and son and made the crossing, along with a few head of his prized cattle." He paused. "It takes a lot of courage to set off into the unknown, to do something entirely new with only yourself to count on."

"Courage . . . or desperation," she said quietly.

What desperation had driven her from wherever home had been? So many times he'd been tempted to ask her point-blank. But he reined in his impatience, telling himself if he wanted to know the full story, he'd have to wait for her to tell him in her own time.

Thinking of the sparks that had struck between them when he took her hand, he was more and more certain that eventually, she would.

Chapter Nine

AFTER ANOTHER TEN minutes' slow drive down the dirt trail, they reached the cabin. Mary had been veering from anticipation back to apprehension at the idea of spending the day with Brice. Predictably—and annoyingly—after the warmth and enjoyment of the evening they'd cooked dinner together, when she'd decided maybe she was ready to explore a relationship with someone, she'd awakened the next morning alarmed and conflicted. Not sure attempting that was a good idea, but locked into the outing, she'd impulsively agreed to attend.

She'd arrived at Elaine's house uncomfortable and tense. The half hour or so of banter between Brice and their friends had recaptured the warmth and ease of their cooking episode, relaxing her again.

Then he'd helped her up into his truck, and the touch of his hand had sent a jolt of physical awareness through her.

Apparently, that initial awakening of her senses she'd felt in the library wasn't going to go away. If anything, the attraction grew stronger every time she saw him. Complicating that was the fact that she really liked Brice McAllister.

What was she going to do about it?

The drive out, with Brice and Bunny chatting, gave her time to relax again. *It'll be fine*, she told herself. *It would have been silly and cowardly to back out at the last minute, just because there was a change in plans. You'll get to see the cabin and some beautiful ranch land, and get to know Brice better. He hasn't pushed you for more than you're willing to give. You don't need to either retreat or force things. Just let it happen naturally.*

She was still repeating that last part as a mantra when they reached the cabin.

Abby's van was already parked behind the house, and she walked out to meet them, Katie skipping at her side.

"Welcome, everyone," Abby said. "Bunny, you've already seen the cabin. Do you want to color with Katie on the back deck? She brought extra pictures and markers for you."

"C'mon, Bunny," Katie said. "Mommy drew me a whole set of princess pictures to color."

While the two girls scampered off, Brice took the picnic basket from the truck and followed the two women. "Grant wanted furnishings that left the cabin still looking like a cabin, but comfortable, easy to live with and clean," Abby was telling Mary. "We've been real happy with it."

Mary followed her hostess through the entry door and stopped short, surprise and admiration replacing the anxious thoughts in her brain.

She'd entered from a portico-sheltered porch into a wide, open one-room space. To the left of the door was a farm table surrounded by whitewashed chairs, with an old buffet displaying linens and wineglasses, hung on rake heads mounted to the buffet's back. To the right, forming most of the wall and flanked by double windows on one side, French doors on the other, a large fireplace made of golden, Hill Country limestone dominated the space. Arranged in front of it were a tan leather couch flanked by two overstuffed chairs covered in a denim fabric, the area defined by a patterned rug in tones of rust, tan, and blue. The kitchen, straight across the room from the entry, had a long island with a stone countertop, the base of it covered in roofing tin, which also formed the backsplash above the kitchen counters. Storage was a combination of cabinets with chicken-wire-fronted doors and open shelving.

"Wow, this is magnificent," Mary said, truly awed. "The shop was impressive enough, but seeing all these designs together in a unified whole—just wow."

"Grant wanted a place where he could come home after chasing cows or mowing and be able to put his feet up and relax without worrying about getting something dirty or messing something up. So the walking space is broad, the wood-look tile floors easy to clean, as are the denim covers on the chairs. And he can put his boots up on the coffee table—it's made from a watering trough, with a wooden top."

Mary had thought decor using found materials, tin, chicken wire, and a chandelier that looked like it was made of branding irons, would create a style too rustic or primitive to appeal to her—but somehow, it hadn't. Instead, it looked more like a western twist on modern industrial. Everywhere she looked was another innovative use of some material or object.

"Told you she was a creative genius," Brice said.

"You are that!" Mary agreed.

"Thanks," Abby said, pinking a little at their praise. "I'm so pleased you like it. Now, we'd better have lunch so I can get the girls back to the showroom. My sister-in-law Marge is dropping Sissie off while she does some shopping. I'll take all the girls back into town and leave Katie and Sissie to overnight at Marge's with their friend, Jillee. Marge wanted to give me and Grant some 'honeymoon time,'" Abby added, her blush deepening.

"Since you never really took one," Brice said.

"No place else I'd rather be than here," she said simply. "Let's enjoy that picnic! I brought some of Katie's lemonade."

They walked out through the French doors beside the fireplace to the deck, with its expansive view across the valley to a series of hills. Mary thought she saw the twinkling reflections of a river in the narrow canyon at the foot of the hill.

"This is 'wow' too," she marveled. "What a magnificent view!"

"You can see why Grant wanted to refurbish the old cabin," Brice said.

"Yes! With this vista, it would be hard to even consider living anywhere else. I can see why you never want to leave, Abby."

At a picnic table on the deck, the girls were busy coloring, while several Adirondack chairs lined up adjoining it, positioned for maximum enjoyment of the view. Looking up at the adults as they walked out, Bunny said, "Can we have our lunch now?"

"Nothing like a hungry six-year-old to bring you back to the practical," Mary said to Brice. Turning to Bunny, she said, "What's your most favoritest food in the whole world?"

Bunny paused, frowning. "The cheese we cut this morning. Or maybe tomatoes."

"How about you, Katie?"

"I love cheese too."

"Good, because we're going to make bruschetta. You put the tomatoes and cheese on the Italian bread we toasted, sprinkle with some balsamic vinegar, and add some fresh basil on the top. Or you can eat the tomatoes and cheese and bread by themselves. We brought some sliced ham. So you can make a sandwich, too, if you prefer."

Bunny paused, obviously considering the bruschetta combination with suspicion. "I want the cheese and bread and tomatoes by themselves."

"Me, too," Katie echoed.

"Okay. Remember, we have olives and sliced cucumbers

and green peppers from the garden too," Mary said as she unpacked the basket onto the picnic table.

"Girls, let me take your pictures and crayons to put back in the van. Brice, why don't you help me bring out the lemonade and the glasses?" Abby said.

After Abby gathered up the art supplies, while she and Brice went back into the cabin to get the drinks, Mary helped the two girls assemble plates of cheese, tomatoes, and bread. After saying a quick grace, she let them plunge in.

"I didn't make them wait," she said as Abby and Brice came back out, Brice bearing a tray with the glasses. "I hope you don't mind."

Abby laughed. "Not at all. I learned early never to stand between that girl and her food."

"The adults have the same options. Bruschetta, or you can make a regular sandwich with bread, meat, and cheese. I have mayo and mustard as well as the balsamic vinegar."

"Bruschetta for sure," Abby said as Grant added, "Same for me."

"This is delicious!" Abby exclaimed after her first bite.

"It's the homegrown tomatoes and fresh basil," Mary said.

"Whatever, the combination is wonderful," Brice said.

"Text me sometime when you're free, Mary," Abby said between bites. "I make a run into the post office or UPS to mail items several times a week. We could meet for lunch or coffee."

"I should make an appointment to come out to shop, make those canning-jar pendant lights." She might not be sure what she wanted to do about Brice McAllister, but she definitely wanted to develop her friendship with this talented lady.

"Yes, we should do that too."

Abby had barely finished her first slice of bruschetta when Katie said, "I'm done now, Mommy. Can we go? I don't want Aunt Marge and Sissie to have to wait on us."

Putting down her half-empty glass with a rueful smile, Abby said, "No, that wouldn't be polite, would it? Well, girls, are you ready?"

"We have more pictures to color back at our house," Katie told Bunny. "Maybe we can even use some of Mommy's paints."

"You can use whatever supplies you want," Abby confirmed.

"Yeah, paints!" Bunny cried. "Yes, I'm ready, Miss Abby."

"Race you to the van," Katie said to Bunny, and then the little girls were off running.

Shaking her head, Abby said, "Take your time and enjoy the scenery. Grant will be back midafternoon, so you don't need to worry about locking up."

"Thank you for letting me see the cabin. It's inspiring."

Waving a hand toward the distant hills and canyons, Abby said, "*That* was inspiring. The colors of tan and ochre and dusty green, the clear blue of the water below. All the colors I wanted to bring inside to reflect the beauty outside."

"You certainly succeeded!"

"Thanks," Abby said with a smile. "I'll be expecting a text setting up a get-together."

"You'll have one soon," Mary promised.

"Don't bother walking me out." Abby waved them back down as Mary and Brice stood. "I've got two impatient little girls waiting and need to hustle. Finish your bruschetta and lemonade. See you later, Brice."

"You, too, Abby."

HER INITIAL NERVOUSNESS at being alone with Brice quelled by the lazy camaraderie of lunch and the beautiful scenery, Mary told herself to just relax. The picnic would be topped by a tour of the ranch. If the rest of it was as beautiful as this place, she could understand why the McAllisters were so attached to their land.

While she gazed around, Brice was assembling another bruschetta. "In case I missed telling you emphatically enough, this is great!"

Mary nodded, pleased he liked it. "It was one of the first things my *nonna* taught me to make. I always smile and think of her when I bite into the crusty bread, with the smooth taste of mozzarella cheese, the sweet tomato, tangy basil, and the bite of the vinegar."

"Do you see her often?" Brice asked.

His question shocked her into realizing that, relaxed and with her guard down, she'd let slip the first thing about her past she'd ever revealed to anyone in Whiskey River. After an initial jolt of alarm, she told herself it was silly to be concerned. Up until now she'd avoided talking about her family because thinking about the past hurt too much, but some memories, like those of her grandmother, were only sweet.

No reason she couldn't share those—without giving anything else away.

"I wish I could," she replied at last. "I lost her when I was sixteen. I miss her terribly—she was the one who taught me to cook, emphasized how much better food tasted when it came directly from your garden into the kitchen. Instilled a love of gardening I still carry with me." Enough sharing; determined to direct the conversation away from her before he could use her confidence to ask any more questions, she said, "What about you? Do you still have your grandparents with you?"

"Sadly, no. Granddaddy—my daddy's father—died the winter before Daddy did. He'd still been helping out on the ranch almost right up to the end, but after my grandma died, he . . . just drifted away. It was hard times then, with beef prices way down and grain prices high. Daddy did more of the work himself, spending long hours out in the fields in all weather. He got sick—just a cold, he told us boys. Wouldn't see a doctor or slow down. Turns out the 'cold' was pneumonia, and by the time we finally realized how sick he was, he could hardly breathe. Seems like he was sick, and then gone so quickly, we couldn't believe what had happened."

Brice blew out a breath. "I still feel guilty that we didn't realize how seriously ill he was, didn't do more to help him around the ranch. Just dumb kids, all wrapped up in ourselves and school—I was playing junior high football then and had just discovered girls. Makes me ashamed to remember how much we groused about the chores he did ask us to do. Then he was just . . . gone."

Like Ian, Mary thought. One minute vibrant, laughing, the center of her world. Then . . . gone.

"I'm sorry. It must have been terrible." She knew only too well how terrible.

Brice nodded. "Bad for us, but my stepmom, Miss Dorothy, felt even more guilty. I think that's why she moved back to San Antonio as soon as Duncan finished college and came back to run the ranch. Her guilt over not recognizing how sick Daddy was, and her sense of failure at having had to sell off land while we were in high school to meet payments on the loans Daddy had taken out when times were good. She knew Duncan hated losing any part of the Triple A and felt she'd let all of us down."

"Did Duncan resent it?" she asked, wondering if those problems had caused a rift in his family. Family rifts being another thing she knew all too much about.

"Duncan hated selling off land, but he didn't blame Miss Dorothy for it. Things were bad for all the ranchers then. She always felt, if she'd been a man with a better understanding of ranching, she might have been able to find some other way to raise the money. Whether that's true or not, I've no idea, but we've all tried to tell her that none of it was her fault. She knows we love her, and is always happy to see us when we visit her condo in San Antonio, but . . . she won't come back to live in Whiskey River, despite how much we've urged her."

"Too many bitter memories," Mary said softly. She could understand that too.

"Too many bitter memories, I guess," Brice agreed. "But eventually Duncan recovered the section of land she had to sell, so all is well again with the world."

"And Miss Dorothy is happy in her new life?"

"Yes. She'd lived in the city before Daddy asked her to come take care of us after Mama died. She never complained about living on a ranch with nothing but work and few leisure activities, but I think she was happy to get back to the city. She has her circle of friends, restaurants, music, shopping. There's a lingering sadness, I think, but basically, she's happy."

Maybe there was hope for her, too, Mary thought. In this new life in a new place. Would she end up settled, content, like Brice's stepmother, only a "lingering sadness" to remind her of all she had lost?

Would her shrunken heart expand to be able to include someone else, someone new, in that world? To make the new world fuller and more complete?

Realizing she'd been sitting silent, she looked up to see Brice watching her.

Could she include that man?

She looked away quickly, afraid her expression might reveal her longing. "Would you like more cheese or tomatoes?" she asked.

"I think I'm done. Are you ready to go see the ranch?"

Some of her misgivings returned. "I'm eager to see the Triple A. But I'm not nearly as excited to meet my equine partner as Bunny would have been."

"Don't be worried. Snowflake is as gentle and easygoing a horse as you could imagine. Abby hadn't been on a horse for a long time, either. Grant started her out on Snowflake and she loved it."

"I'm counting on your love of Italian cooking to make sure nothing bad happens to me. Like falling off into a cactus or down a ravine."

"Making sure nothing bad happens to you is one of my goals in life," he said lightly. But something in his tone and his expression as he said it sent a little jolt through her.

He wanted . . . to look out for her? The thought sent a rush of warmth and appreciation through her. He'd make a formidable defender.

But better not let herself start leaning on him. If losing

Ian had taught her anything, it was she could never rely on having someone else in her life to make her happy or solve her problems.

Though getting closer to him was appealing. When she relaxed, enjoying a bantering conversation, it was all too easy to indulge the sensual attraction that had surprised her that first day at the library, and that hummed in her veins every time she saw him. That prompted her to want to take things further.

Until she remembered the inevitable stumbling block.

He was a healthy young male, and in today's world, getting much closer would lead to expectations of intimacy. An intimacy she couldn't allow herself.

Better just to remain acquaintances with a common friend—Bunny.

A SHORT TIME later, having put their glasses in the dishwasher and stowed away the trash, Mary followed Brice back to the truck. "Will we see the cows on the way to the barn?" she asked, trying to distract herself from the idea of riding.

"No, they're in the west pasture, down by the river where the grass is better. It gets pretty dry on the ridges by this time of year," he explained.

"Will there be calves with them?"

"There aren't any new babies," Brice told her. "The

calves are all born in the spring, so by now they're all pretty big."

Mary looked over in surprise. "How do you get them all to be born at the same time?"

Brice laughed. "There's a lot of work to birth, tag, brand, and then nurture both the calves and their mommas. It's more efficient if all the cows are on the same schedule, so we know when to look for offspring and can do big jobs like vaccinating and branding all at once, rather than over and over throughout the year. So the herd bulls are only put in the pasture with the cows for about two-and-a-half months over the summer, which will result in the calves being dropped during a ninety-day period from February through April."

"That makes sense. Sorry for the dumb questions. I told you I didn't know anything about ranching."

"Not dumb at all. Duncan would appreciate your interest." He chuckled. "But like Tom advised, don't ask him any ranching questions unless you are really interested. He's normally not long-winded, but the Triple A is his passion. Ask about cattle breeding procedures and you could be trapped for a long time. When it involves ranching, he could talk the hide off a cow."

"I'll keep that in mind."

She hadn't initially wanted to get closer to Brice McAllister. But she had to admit, his calm, competent, nonthreatening presence, the strong sense of family love and loyalty evident when he talked about his brothers and the Triple A, appealed to something deep within her. That longing for the family she'd lost, perhaps? The sense of belonging, being a part of a chain of people you love?

"We're pulling up at the Scott ranch house now," Brice told her. "Grant wants to bring Snowflake, Moondust, and his gelding out to the cabin eventually, but he has to build a barn first. So for now, he leaves them here. Besides, the horse barn is at the center of the property, which makes it easy to ride in either direction."

"Isn't this the barn that he's renovating?"

"No, that's the equipment barn. The horse barn will stay. Need a place for the horses to be when kids or other groups come up for ranching days."

"Makes sense. Which direction will we ride in?"

"You've seen Grant's cabin, which is along the eastern border of the Triple A. We're now at the center. I thought we'd ride to the west, to where the McAllister house and barns are, then down to the meadows by the river to see the cows. There's also a sharp bend in the river there that has lots of rocks to climb—or collect to decorate your garden."

"Sounds good," Mary said, still trying to quell her nervousness about the prospect of getting on horseback.

She mustn't have succeeded in masking her anxiety, for Brice gave her a reassuring smile. "Don't worry, you'll be fine."

"Right. Like sitting in a rocking chair," Mary said wryly.

"It will be. I'll keep the pace very slow. You'll have to keep talking to me, so I don't go to sleep and fall off my horse."

"Why do I not find that prospect reassuring?" she said wryly, while he laughed.

After Brice parked the truck, they walked to the paddock fence, where a pretty silver-gray pony with a dark mane and tail lifted her head at their approach. "That's Moondust, of the sore hoof," Brice said, leaning over to give the pony a pat. "Hope you feel better soon, little gal." Turning back to Mary, he said, "I'll get our horses tacked up and ready."

Mary nodded, then watched him walk into the paddock and grab the halters of the other two horses, a tall chestnut with a snowy white blaze on her forehead and an even taller black one.

"Please tell me mine is the smaller one—although neither one looks like 'Snowflake' would be a fitting name."

"The black gelding that I'll ride is 'Lightfoot,' named by Harrison's dad because he picks up his feet like a dancer—and loves to gallop. This little lady is 'Snowflake,' for the white blaze on her forehead."

"I earnestly hope she's a well-mannered lady, but there's no way I'd call her 'little.'"

"She's a sweetheart, though. And don't worry. I'll take care of you."

There it was again—the statement that he'd watch out for her. A deep-seated need to protect women, Elaine had told her, born of the inability to help his stepmother when times were bad on the ranch? After what he'd told her today, she could believe it.

She had to admit, it felt . . . reassuring to be the focus of all that competent protectiveness.

She followed him into the barn. Teasing and joking to keep her distracted, Brice got the horses saddled, then helped Mary mount the mare. "If you'd feel better, I can lead her," he said.

"Probably makes me look like a wuss, but I'd prefer that," Mary admitted.

But after five minutes of walking down the trail from the barn, Mary started to relax. Snowflake really was easygoing, with a smooth gait that didn't bounce her around too much once she got the hang of being in the saddle. After another five minutes, she relaxed enough to begin to enjoy the scenery.

"Riding is the best way to see the ranch," she said. "A whole 360-degree vista all around you, instead of just what can be seen out the windows of the truck."

"Horses also go where trails and vehicles can't," Brice said. "Lots of places on the ranch are easier to ride to than drive. Though we don't use horses for the ranch work anymore. If we're hunting strays in an area that's too hilly or rocky, we just have to drive as close as we can and then walk from there."

"Do cows stray? I thought they stayed with the herd."

"Normally they do. But when a mama cow is ready to calf, she sometimes goes off on her own. And sometimes one will just get a hankering to see what's on the other side of the fence."

"To see if the grass really is greener?" Mary suggested with a smile.

"Okay, walked into that one," Brice said, chuckling.

After another ten-minute ride, she could see down the lane in the distance a sprawling ranch house. "That's the ranch house for the Triple A," Brice confirmed.

"Where you grew up?"

"Yes. Duncan's done some renovations over the years to bring it into the twenty-first century. Looked pretty much like a magazine spread for the 1950s when we were growing up. Daddy never had much extra cash for things like modernizing kitchens or bathrooms. And in true rancher fashion, he'd rather be out on the meadow, mowing or working cows, than indoors anyway. So he didn't pay much attention to décor. As long as the electricity and plumbing worked, that was good enough for him."

"I don't imagine you and your brothers cared much about style either."

"Not growing up. I think the outmoded house was one reason why Miss Dorothy was happy to get back to the city. Once Duncan moved back after college, he had to replace some appliances that had died, which started him on some painting and refinishing. Gotta say, the place looks much better now, and Harrison's beginning to add her own touches. Maybe I can show you around sometime."

Mary made a noncommittal murmur. She was warming, vacillating between keep-it-acquaintances and becoming closer friends, but didn't want to commit herself to anything yet.

They passed the house, then turned onto a narrow dirt lane that led across the plateau and steadily downward. In a pasture bordered by a small meandering river, Mary saw a herd of perhaps fifty cows.

"Can we go in and see them?" Mary asked.

"Might not be a good idea. The mamas can be very protective of their calves. Normally, they are docile folks, but if one took it into her head that you were a threat to her baby, she might charge you. But we can rein in so you can watch them."

They halted for a few minutes, Brice giving her a brief rundown of the cows, their calves, and the care the ranch gave them. Then they continued down the trail to where the land flattened out to a broad space. The river curved sharply here, leaving a section of boulders tumbled against each other as if tossed there by a playful giant.

Pulling up his horse, which made her mount obligingly stop, Brice said, "We'll dismount and let the horses graze. My brothers and I used to climb the rocks over by the creek, skip stones, and otherwise steal a little time to goof off when we were supposed to be tending fences or mowing."

"It's a pretty spot. And the river is beautiful."

He helped her dismount. Her legs felt a little funny, but she managed to stay upright.

"Okay?" he asked, giving her a steadying hand. "Your knees can feel a little shaky after getting out of the saddle if you're not used to riding."

"I'm okay," she managed to croak out of a suddenly tight throat. It was the touch of his hand making her feel weak-kneed, leaving her both disappointed and relieved when he removed his support.

"So, how did you like your first ride?"

"I liked it," she said, realizing she meant it. "Of course, my protector was keeping me safe."

"Always. Do you want to climb the rocks? If not, you can sit over here—we used to picnic on that big flat rock—or wander around and fill your bucket with whichever rocks you want to take back to your garden."

"I can really take some rocks back? The golden stone is so beautiful!"

"We only charge by the ton. Help yourself. I'm going to climb to the top. Sort of a ritual. Every time I come here, I have to climb to the top."

"Used to be a race with your brothers?" she guessed.

"Exactly. A king-of-the-mountain thing."

"I'll let you play that one alone. But I will rest here a bit before I collect the rocks."

"Take your time." Nodding to her, he headed toward the

tumbled boulders.

Sighing, Mary settled on the big rock. She watched Brice appear and disappear as he threaded his way upward on the boulders then closed her eyes and turned her face up into an early fall sun that was warming but not oppressive.

She let her mind drift to a blank, her senses focused on the trickling sound of the water, the soft breeze, the sigh of the wind through the grasses and the leaves of the river birches bordering the stream on the far side. Finding peace, tranquility, and calm—everything she'd been seeking when she left her childhood home.

Was she finally ready to share her life with someone else again? With a man who let her go at her own pace, who didn't push, who was a strong, quiet, supportive presence?

Maybe it *was* time to let go of the past. She'd come here to build a new life. Could Brice McAllister be part of it?

Would he want to be?

By the time Brice climbed back down, Mary had shaken herself out of her pleasant haze and collected a dozen beautiful, golden rocks for her garden. When they saddled up to ride back to the Scott barn, she was feeling confident enough to hold the reins herself, earning an approving nod from Brice.

"We'll make you a cowgirl yet, library lady."

"I'm not quite ready to rodeo," she said drily.

"You've got a natural feel for it—seem to instinctively relax and let your body go with the horse. My brother Grant is best of us at that. He was a saddle bronc rider in high school. Could find the rhythm on any horse he drew, which resulted in him being state champion two years running. I'm good, but not that good. But don't ever tell him I said that."

She drew a line over her lips with her finger. "Mum's the word."

But his gaze fastened on her mouth made it tingle. How would it feel if he kissed her?

Shocked, she looked away. The idea of kissing someone hadn't entered her mind in ages. She really must be coming out of that state of frozen animation she'd lived in the last three years.

It would be good to enjoy companionship, attraction. But some of the broken things in her life couldn't be fixed by peace and serenity. Those things might make it impossible to establish a relationship with any man. Especially one as virile and attractive as Brice McAllister.

She was still marveling at her reaction when they reached the barn. Brice helped her dismount—making her arms prickle with awareness when he helped her down. That feeling setting off a melting sensation in her belly, she stood by the fence as Brice put away the tack and groomed the horses before turning them out into the paddock again.

Still unsettled by the strength of her sensual awakening, Mary didn't want to make idle conversation on the ride back to town. Fortunately, Brice seemed okay with silence.

A short time later, he parked the truck in front of her

cottage. "Safely home, my lady. With no bumps or bruises, even after the ride."

He paused, as if he wanted to say something else. Like offer to come in for a glass of wine?

Did she dare invite him?

Before she could decide whether to take the plunge, he'd come to her side of the truck to help her down. Her gaze caught on his blue, blue eyes and she felt again that thrilling, alarming urge to kiss him.

Resisting it, she looked away and took his hand, her fingers tingling.

"Lunch was great." Brice retrieved her picnic basket from the back of his truck. "You enjoyed the riding, too, didn't you?"

"Yes, it was wonderful," she said, surprised to realize she meant it.

"Thanks for coming along," Brice said. "I really enjoyed showing you around the Triple A."

"It was my pleasure." Better bid him goodbye before she confused herself any more. "Good night, then. Thanks again for asking me."

"It was *my* pleasure."

Conscious of his gaze following her, she walked up her front steps, unlocked the door and stepped inside, giving him a little wave after she'd turned the lights on. After waving back, he returned to the driver's side and hopped back into his truck.

She watched as he drove away, feeling a mingling of relief that she hadn't done something stupid—like ask him in for wine and invite an intimacy she didn't dare initiate—and regret that she had to be wise.

But a soft voice inside was insisting he was too good an opportunity to pass up. That she might not want to be just friends. That she should make the effort to find out.

Starting a new life, as they'd agreed, meant she would have to take chances.

Chapter Ten

THE NEXT MORNING, Brice was up early, taking a cup of coffee out onto the back porch of the Scott ranch house, gazing at the calming vista of mist rising off the distant creek.

He'd had lots of time last night to think about the day and how to proceed from there. Mary seemed at times more relaxed, other times tense—like when he touched her. Which confirmed the sparks he felt were mutual. And that she was uneasy about it.

If she had been in an abusive relationship, she might be wary of physical intimacy. Though there was nothing he wanted more now than to hold her, kiss her, make love to her, he knew more patience was required to let her become fully comfortable with him. Push her too fast, and like a half-broke colt, she'd dump him off and bolt for the hills.

He'd never had to be this cautious with a lady before. Usually, if he confirmed there was mutual interest, they'd go quickly from first contact to friendship to something more, or after a few dates, decide to part friends. After his initial few years in college, when he'd been content with revolving-door physical relationships with equally freewheeling women, he was no longer satisfied with just a physical hookup. He wanted to be at least friends. His last two relationships, he now realized, he'd been looking for "more" and hadn't found it, which was why those relationships had ended.

And Ashley's two-timing, of course. Which had made him skeptical of a woman's promises and doubtful about her ability to keep them.

When he thought of Mary, he didn't feel that wariness. She was so cautious herself, he'd bet she'd never commit to anything unless she was totally, absolutely sure.

Nor had he ever had to wait long for physical intimacy, if the attraction was mutual. He had to admit, he wasn't looking forward to abstinence around a woman he wanted to kiss every time he saw her. But he could control his desire, because the sparks that fizzed between them when they touched promised the eventual passion would be powerful and well worth the wait.

Now, the question he'd been wrestling with. He'd been using Bunny as a shield to ease Mary into knowing him better. He was pretty sure she now trusted him enough that if trouble came, she would call on him. So he's accomplished his initial mission.

But sometime during that mission, his objective had changed. He no longer just wanted to make sure she was protected, he wanted to spend time with her. He liked how he felt when he was around her—grounded, at peace, content. He liked watching her—those lovely dark eyes, her capable hands, and her generous, giving spirit as she entertained Bunny. He liked being with her, doing simple things, like picking vegetables or simmering homemade tomato sauce.

Who would have thought the swinging bachelor would be stopped in his tracks by a homebody who loved to cook and garden?

He wasn't ready to print the engagement announcements yet, but he was determined to continue his slow, easy wooing and see where it led. Because if it led to a lifetime with Mary, he might just be happy enough to drop that harp through a cloud.

Was it even possible?

At some point, she would have to trust him enough to move beyond seeing him with Bunny.

He was encouraged that she hadn't pulled out of the ranch trip after she learned Bunny wouldn't be with them all day—but there had been the incentive of seeing the cabin. And she'd seemed to enjoy herself, becoming nervous again only occasionally. But he'd never yet asked her to accompany him alone, just the two of them from start to finish.

Maybe it was time to test those waters.

He debated calling her, then decided to text instead. It would give her time to think over what he was asking, not put her on the spot for an immediate answer.

He had the feeling that if she were forced to reply right

then and there, she'd panic and turn him down.

Taking a deep breath, telling himself not to be too discouraged if he got a negative answer, he texted, *Hey, Brice here. Had a great day yesterday. Know you enjoy wine. Hill Country Oktoberfest next weekend. There are tickets for a bus to take you to ones you want, so don't have to drive, dinner afterward before the drive home. One winery boasts 'Super Texan,' supposed to compare to Super Tuscans, my SIL, Harrison says. Like to go?*

He re-read the screen, debating, then thought, *What the hell. Time to fish or cut bait*, and hit "send."

HE WAS DRIVING out to another small town today to talk with the bank manager in relation to his bank fraud investigation. He kept glancing at his phone, but by midday, he still hadn't heard back from Mary.

That was good news, he encouraged himself. If she was going to refuse, he would have heard back already. So she must at least be debating accepting.

It wasn't until later that afternoon, as he was driving back after finding one promising "questionable" transaction, that he finally heard the ping announcing a text. Too anxious to wait, he pulled over to the side of the road. His hands were actually shaking as he swiped open the phone to read her reply.

Thanks for the invite. Sounds like fun. When and where?

He sat back in his seat, giddily delighted. *Hot damn, maybe this was going somewhere after all.* He blew out a deep breath, telling himself to resist the impulse to text back immediately, like he'd been waiting all day for her response—even though he had. That might seem too much like pressure.

He'd text her when he got back to the ranch. Then call Harrison, his go-to for wine expertise, and start planning for a day Mary couldn't help enjoying.

THE FOLLOWING SATURDAY morning, Brice was up early at the ranch, enthused by anticipation of the day to come and encouraged by the progress they were making on the bank fraud case. He'd gradually been narrowing the net on which of several banks harbored the insider who was arranging the fraudulent transactions. And as in the past, Brice was pretty confident that sooner or later, greed, inattention, or a simple mistake would make the perpetrator slip up and give them the clue they needed to identify and prosecute the culprit.

Too early to leave, too antsy to sit still, he'd go to the barn and visit the horses. Then come back, shower, put on his "going out" boots and jeans and favorite shirt for luck.

After stopping by the kitchen to grab some apples, he strode out to the paddock. The horses turned at his approach, nickered in greeting, and ambled over immediately.

"Yeah, you smell those apples from a mile away, don't you girl," he crooned, rubbing Snowflake's blaze while he fed her the apple—she being the one the others deferred to for treats first. Then with an apple in each hand, he fed Moondust and Lightfoot. Apples consumed, the two mares wandered off, but Lightfoot, his usual mount, lingered while Brice rubbed his neck in the place he most liked.

"Got a major test today, Big Guy," he said. "I'm making a move on that gal, but it has to be the right one. Smooth and steady and graceful, like your gait. Cause she might be the one, and I don't want to blow this. But don't you tell Grant that. I'd never hear the end of it. The swinging bachelor, falling in love at last."

The words that seemed to tumble out without thought brought him up short. Was he falling in love with Mary?

He didn't know. He just knew he wanted to be with her, wanted to know everything about her and the mysterious past she never discussed, wanted to protect her. Wanted her to trust him and rely on him.

He also knew he'd never felt as intense a desire to be emotionally and physically close to a woman as he felt around Mary.

Maybe he was falling. Surprisingly, that thought didn't arouse the anxiety he would have anticipated, wary as he'd been after Ashley's betrayal.

Sometimes as boys, he and his brothers would take old tractor inner tubes down to the creek, hop in and let the current carry them along, content to ride until they ran aground or decided to go home. Serene, quiet, no pressure.

Which is how this relationship would have to be. He'd do all he could to put his best foot forward, then wade into the creek and see where the ride took him.

TWO HOURS LATER, Brice parked his truck by the car in Mary's driveway. Elaine, Tom and Bunny were away for the weekend, which meant they'd not have to dodge having their "bestest" friend want to come along with them.

Just the two of them—for the first time since that frosty meeting in the library.

Thinking of the library, he frowned. He sure hoped Mary wasn't going to wear another of her ugly dresses. But then, if she did, he wouldn't have to worry about other guys ogling her, he thought with a chuckle.

Then he caught sight of her as she answered the door and his tongue stuck to the roof of his suddenly dry mouth.

She looked beautiful, her dark hair pinned partially up in the front, left down in the back in a glossy tangle of curls. Red lipstick outlined lips that practically demanded "kiss me," a sleeveless red blouse in some sort of silky material floated over her torso, its deep vee hinting at her lush cleavage, and she wore narrow, black pencil trousers that accentuated her long legs.

When she said, "Hi to you, too, Brice," a little nervously, he realized he'd been just standing there, gaping.

"You look gorgeous. Or especially gorgeous," he corrected, exasperated at his clumsiness as she stood aside to let him walk in. "You look wonderful all the time."

To his relief, she laughed. "Even in my Old Maid Librarian dresses?"

"If you think they look like that, why—?" He stopped himself. "So they are a disguise. The dresses and the glasses. To present a nondescript image and keep people from looking closer."

She nodded. "Mostly just to keep men from looking closer."

He waited hopefully, but she added nothing further, saying, "I hope this outfit is okay for winetasting. I didn't know how uneven the terrain would be, so I wore pants and sensible shoes."

"Most of the places have paved lots and sidewalks, so the terrain shouldn't be a problem. And thanks for not wearing your Old Maid Librarian dress. Which means—you trust me, right?"

"I have to admit, I had one of the dresses laid out to wear," she confessed. "Then I thought you'd already seen me in short shorts and a halter top, so that horse was already out of the barn. A good Texas expression, right?"

"I approve. The question remains—do you approve? Of me?"

"I wouldn't have agreed to go to the festival if I hadn't decided that I could trust you."

Brice felt an enormous rush of relief and a deep sense of gratitude. "I'll take that as a huge compliment."

"You should. It's been a very, very long time since I trusted anyone of the male gender. But I told myself that if I'm ever to stop just existing, I have to have the courage to move on." She gave him an uneasy smile. "I've bet on you to help me."

Floored, grateful, Brice promised, "I'll do anything I can. Since I don't know what demons you are fighting, I don't know what to encourage or what to avoid. If I stray into stressful territory, assume it's unintentional and tell me to stop."

"I can do that."

And in time, I hope, trust me enough to tell me the whole.

"Ready?"

She nodded. "Along with sunscreen and bug spray, I packed a thermos of espresso, some Parmesan crisps and some flat Italian crackers that I like. They are good complements to many types of wine."

She picked up a large tote bag from the floor. Brice felt absurdly gratified when, after he held out his arm with a questioning look, she allowed him to take it. Daring to put a hand at the small of her back, he escorted her out to the truck.

After stowing the bag, he offered a hand to help her

climb up the high step. This time, looking at him steadily, a slight smile on her face, she took his hand, clasping it firmly in hers.

Tingling sensations coursed from the pressure of her fingers all through his body. His heart rate soared and for a moment, he forgot to breathe. Then, with one of those wonderful smiles she usually reserved for Bunny, she said, "Going to help me up?"

Belatedly remembering what he was supposed to be doing, he nodded, then gave her an assist.

He shook his head as he walked back to the driver's side of the truck.

If she affected him that much, just pressing his hand, his heart might not stand the excitement of full intimacy. But, being a brave soul, he'd be ready and willing to try.

They were a far piece and a county away from that yet. But having her not just acknowledge, but seem to accept, the sensual attraction between them was an enormous step.

And a perfect beginning to the day.

As they drove along, she said, "I checked into how the festival works. We park in Fredericksburg, then take a minivan out to the wineries, right?"

"Normally it works like that, but the regular tours don't make any distinction between people getting their first taste of wine, those who know a lot about it, and the younger set that just wants to party. I talked with my sister-in-law Harrison, who's really knowledgeable about local wines. She made me a list of the ones she thought someone who likes Italian wine would find interesting, then arranged through a friend who knows a friend to have a driver take us just to those places. Two this morning, two this afternoon, rather than the tour that might do quick stops at three or more places morning and afternoon. I hope that will be enough."

"That will be perfect! I want time to savor and appreciate. I never want to feel the effects of the alcohol wine contains, so I limit how much I drink. And I drink it because I love the taste of ones I choose and how they complement what I cook. On the few occasions when I open something I've never had before and don't like the taste, I give it away."

"After the tours, we'll have dinner in Fredericksburg. There are lots of great restaurants. You can choose from traditional barbecue to German—the early residents of town were of Germanic heritage—to Mexican salsa. There are Italian places, but after eating in your kitchen, nothing would compare. After a couple of hours over a leisurely dinner with soda water, it will be safe for me to drive back."

"Sounds perfect."

They chatted the rest of the way about the wines and wineries Harrison had recommended. After arriving on the outskirts of Fredericksburg, Brice eased his truck into one of the municipal lots from which the tour vans departed. "Have you ever been to Fredericksburg?"

She gave him a half smile. "I've kept pretty close to home."

"There's a really nice outdoor museum showcasing early Texas settlement that includes typical houses, a schoolroom, and some display gardens I think you'd enjoy. There's also a great World War II museum here—Admiral Nimitz, one of the heroes of the war in the Pacific, grew up here."

"Nimitz is one of your herd bulls, isn't he?"

"Yes. We actually have Nimitz the Third now. With all the wineries around, Fredericksburg has become a big tourist destination. There are lots of shops and eateries. We can stroll around town before dinner if you like."

"Sounds good. But first, wine."

Brice pulled the truck into a parking spot on the far edge of the lot, away from the spot where the festival vans departed. "We're meeting our driver, Mitch Hannessy, here at the corner," he said as they hopped down and he locked the truck.

"Thank you for arranging this. And for asking me. You must have known I'd debate over whether or not to come. It's too much like a real first date." She shook her head wonderingly. "I haven't been on a 'first date' since I was a teenager."

So whatever relationship she'd lost must have been long term, Brice figured. "We're not calling it a date. It's just an outing with friends doing something they both enjoy."

She laughed. "I did almost turn you down. Then I decided, having met a guy who is courteous, honest, warm, funny and interesting, if I'm not ready to make friends with him, when will I ever be? I've been frozen in the past long enough."

"I'm delighted you're taking a chance on me."

She looked up at him, meeting his gaze. "I hope I will be too," she said softly.

The rest of the day passed as agreeably as Brice had hoped. Their knowledgeable driver gave them some background on the select wineries they stopped at, and his connections with the owners allowed them to have their tastings in smaller, private rooms usually reserved for wine club members.

Brice enjoyed the wine, but even more, he liked watching Mary enjoy it. She got into avid conversations with the baristas serving them about the raising, harvesting, bottling, and aging of the varieties they sampled. She found two wineries with Super Texan blends she liked as much as her Italian Chianti, as well as a lush Petit Syrah and several interesting red blends.

By the end of the afternoon, she'd bought almost a case of wine to add to her wine fridge and joined the wine club at her favorite of the wineries.

They had dinner at a small German restaurant on Fredericksburg's main street after strolling up and down browsing the shops, including some antique boutiques displaying kitchenware like she collected, though she murmured to Brice that the tourist prices were much too high and she'd continue to do her shopping at Old Man Tessel's.

After finishing the event with ice cream from one of the boutiques on the main street, he drove her home, encouraging her to chat about wine and the wineries they'd visited all the way.

Back in Whiskey River, Brice parked his truck beside her car, tension building within him. Would she invite him to come inside? Bid him goodbye at the door? Over the course of the day, she'd been visibly more relaxed—and the subtle glances she gave him when their hands touched or he took her elbow to help her in or out of vehicles said she acknowledged, if not encouraged, the simmering physical connection between them.

He hopped down and went around to help her down, then carried in the several wine bags with the vintages she'd purchased while she brought the tote bag with the empty espresso thermos. As he set the carriers down beside her wine fridge, he said, "Thanks again for going along with me. I probably wouldn't have gone on my own, and I had a fabulous time."

"You could have brought Duncan and Harrison."

"Right, the newlyweds, who probably would have spent the afternoon gazing soulfully into each other's eyes and—" Seeing her smile, he broke off. "Ah, you're teasing me," he realized, totally charmed that she felt comfortable enough to do so.

"How could the day not have been fabulous when I discovered several wonderful new wines? Though my budget may take several months to recover." She paused, a little frown on her face as if debating something. Looking back up, she said, "Would you like an espresso for the road, to keep you alert on the drive to the ranch?"

He nodded. "I'd appreciate it." Even more, he appreciated the offer to let him linger. He had hoped, but not expected it.

"I have some biscotti I baked to go with it. Just a little something light and sweet to complement the tang of the coffee."

"'Tang'? A good description. The first time I had espresso, I nearly choked. Grant had warned me it was 'strong enough to walk into your cup'—another good Texas phrase. Now, I find a lot of restaurant coffee too weak for my taste."

"The Italian blend I buy is definitely not light. Have a seat on the couch and I'll join you in a minute."

Brice went and sat down, heat and anticipation thrumming in his blood. Would this be the night he'd get to kiss her?

He only hoped she'd give him a definite, unmistakable sign if she was ready. He didn't want to forge ahead on a misunderstanding and ruin all the progress toward closeness he'd made today.

The sofa was broad and comfortable. His mind went immediately to kissing her, pressing her back against the overstuffed cushions, tasting her, feeling her heartbeat against his while he explored her mouth . . .

Slow down, cowboy, he told himself. He'd be too heated to drink his coffee.

A minute later, she brought in the tray, wafting the savory aroma of coffee and a hint of sweetness from the biscuits. He drank it and ate the biscotti without really tasting either, all his senses attuned to whether she'd issue that invitation—or not.

Finally, coffee finished and biscuits gone, he had no excuse to delay any longer.

"Guess I'd better hit the road. Thanks again for sharing a perfect day with me."

Only one thing would make it truly perfect, he thought longingly as he set his cup back on the tray.

When he shifted to get up, she stayed him with a touch to his hand. "It was perfect. Thank you," she said. And leaned up and kissed him.

He tried to hold himself absolutely still and let her control the kiss, resist the urgent desire to tease the seal of her lips and slip inside, afire with the need to touch and taste and explore her mouth and tongue. But when she put her hands on either side of his head, a little moan issuing from deep in her throat, he couldn't hold back any longer.

He slid his tongue gently along her lips, probing at the corners of her mouth. When she opened, letting him inside, the jolt of sensation made him dizzy. Then, her hands clutching his head, she was kissing him back with an increasing fervor he was more than happy to match.

He wrapped his arms around her and leaned her back into the nest of cushions, just as he'd dreamed of doing. She continued kissing him ardently, as if starved for sensation. He slid his hands down her sides, massaging her arms, his fingers creeping toward the swell of her breasts when suddenly, she broke off the kiss and pushed at his chest.

Despite his passion-befuddled state, he released her immediately. "What's wrong?"

She put a hand to her mouth, her eyes anguished. "I think you'd better leave. I'm sorry, Brice, but I can't be your good-time girl."

He shook his head, not sure he could be hearing her right. After all his patience and his care, after the cooking and the laughter and the friendship, how could she think that?

"My 'good-time girl'? How can you possibly accuse me of that? Have I ever pressured you for anything? Even hinted that I felt I should get something physical as 'repayment'?"

"Maybe not. But after a certain time in a relationship, most men expect . . . something."

"Well, I'm not 'most men.' And I never, ever take anything a lady isn't more than ready and willing to freely give." Going from frustrated, hurt, and confused to angry, he stood up and collected his hat. "I never wanted or imagined you to be my 'good-time girl.' I thought we had more than that. I guess I thought wrong. Good night, Mary."

He pivoted and stalked out the door.

He was halfway to his truck when Mary came running after him. "Brice—please don't go yet. I owe you an apology—a big apology. And probably, finally, an explanation."

He halted, not turning to look at her, realizing by the depth of the hurt he felt, the anguish and anger about being dismissed so insultingly, he was already much more emotionally involved than was safe with this woman about whom he still knew so little.

But the pleading tone of her voice, and his strong desire to repair the breach that had just been ripped between them, overrode the voice of caution that said it would be smarter to jump in his truck and not look back.

She'd just shown she had the power to inflict some serious damage to his emotions. If he went back, and she walked away again later . . .

Ignoring his misgivings and the voice of self-preservation that was yammering at him to ignore her and leave, he turned to face her.

"Alright. I'll at least listen."

Chapter Eleven

HER BREATH TIGHT in her chest, Mary walked back into the house, conscious of the hurt and angry man following her.

He had a right to be hurt and angry. She'd given him every indication she was ready for the kiss she'd craved ever since admitting to herself that he attracted her as no man had since she'd lost Ian. And for a few wonderful, glorious minutes, she'd let herself go, reveling in the thrill of passion she'd missed for so long she'd hardly been able, before he kissed her, to remember how it felt.

Until his hands began to move, setting off danger warnings in all her senses . . . for she knew if she'd not stopped him then, she might not have been able to resist the overwhelming tide of passion, leading them to do something that would have spelled disaster.

He deserved to know why. She could tell him that much, at least.

As they walked into the kitchen, she said, "I think I need another cup of espresso. Join me?"

His face expressionless, he shook his head, took a seat at

the kitchen island, put his hat on the counter, and waited.

She took as long as possible making the espresso, her hands shaking. Now that she'd resolved to tell him, how did she begin?

Too nervous to sit, she sipped the sharp, strong brew and then took a deep breath. "You already guessed that I'd . . . lost someone. My fiancé, Ian. We were a month from our wedding when we went back to visit a relative in a not-so-great part of the city, just outside downtown L.A. Ian had pulled my brother's car into a parking spot when another car stopped beside ours. Two men with handguns jumped out, fired shots into the car, then sped off. Ian, I found out later, died immediately. I almost did."

"How awful, Mary," he said quietly, compassion replacing his formerly stony expression. "I'm so sorry. Were the shooters ever found?"

She paused, choosing her words carefully before replying, "The police supposed it was a case of mistaken identity in some sort of turf war over drug dealing." Which was the bare truth, if not all of it.

"You recovered, thank heaven."

"After a long time in the hospital. The bullets struck me in the lower abdomen. I was three months pregnant with our child. There was massive hemorrhaging. They kept me sedated in ICU for over a week to control the bleeding, then did surgery to correct the damage. I woke up after surgery to find I'd lost both Ian and the baby. Besides that, the doctors said while it might be possible for me to get pregnant again, because of all the damage and scarring, there was almost no chance I could carry a child to term. Most likely, I would lose it before the child was viable outside the womb."

He shook his head in silent sympathy and reached out to take her trembling hand. Gratefully, she grasped his fingers, forcing herself to go on.

"After I recovered, I couldn't face living in the city anymore, where everywhere I went, there would be memories of what I'd lost. What I could never have. My cousins, with their growing families around them. I went to a school out of state to get my graduate library degree, determined to move as far away as possible. I was just finishing it when the posting came up of a vacancy in Whiskey River. I applied, and they hired me."

Holding tight to her hand, he continued to watch her, the compassion in his gaze making the tears that had already threatened begin slipping down her cheeks.

"When I moved in, I tried to resist Bunny at first. But she's pretty irresistible, as you know. Then I thought, I could enjoy doing things with her that I'll n-never be able to do with a child of my own."

She'd tried to hold it back, but at that admission, the anguish she'd never mastered overwhelmed her. Turning her back on Brice, she put her hands over her eyes and wept.

Desperate to control the flood, she had no awareness of his reaction until she felt strong arms surround her, pulling her gently against his chest. He held her close, murmuring into her hair, not threatening, not demanding, just a solid, steady, reassuring presence.

It took her several minutes to bring herself back under control and step away. Swiping at the tears, she took an unsteady step toward the counter and gulped down more coffee, the sharp jolt of caffeine welcome.

"Sorry," she said, not looking at him. "I usually try not to think about it, since, rather obviously, I . . . haven't stopped grieving. Which brings me to the disaster on the couch. As we've both known for a while, I'm very attracted to you. Kissing you . . . reawakened the passionate side of me I've ignored or stifled since Ian's death. Until the voice of caution reminded me that no birth control method is fail proof, and though I might get pregnant, I could never carry a baby long enough for it to live. One of my cousins had several miscarriages before doctors told her she shouldn't try to get pregnant again. The experience was devastating for her."

"You could do something permanent to prevent pregnancy, couldn't you?"

"You mean a tubal ligation? Yes, I could. Probably I should have, while I was still in the hospital, after the doctors told me what to expect. But as I was recovering, I couldn't face ruling out for good any chance of having a child. Now, after several years, I should probably consider it again."

"I think you've earned the right to take your time about

making such an irreversible decision."

She nodded. "Until you came along, it wasn't a pressing issue. I hadn't even been interested in men . . . before you. And after I met you, and was attracted enough to overcome my strong reservations, a part of me whispered that it was okay to move on with you, okay to taste passion again. But I can't risk it. I can't guarantee I could kiss you and stop short of lovemaking. And I can't face the possibility of conceiving another child I'm destined to lose. Nor would I want to go into a serious relationship with any man, knowing I could never give him children."

She blew out a breath. "I'm sorry I gave you mixed signals. And I especially apologize for my . . . uncalled-for remark. You've been nothing but patient with me from the very beginning." She smiled weakly. "Extremely patient. I really thought you would have given up on me by now."

"I don't want to give up on you," he said quietly. "Thank you for giving me some background. I could tell it wasn't easy to revisit what happened, and I apologize for making you go through it. Time doesn't lessen the grief very much."

"No, it doesn't. So, if you'd rather not see me anymore, knowing now how—limited—I am, I'll understand completely. Which will make this day even more special." She smiled sadly. "A vignette of a memory of how life . . . might have been."

He took her hand again, kissing her fingers before cradling her hand in his big one. "You're not getting rid of me that easily—unless you want me to go. If that's the case, say so clearly, and I'll respect your wishes. Respect them—but that's not what I want. We've just started this Texas two-step of a relationship. Who knows where it might lead? I say we stick with it and find out. And if we both want it to become something more permanent . . . then we'll deal with the issue of children later. No need to push you into any procedures you're not ready to face. And who knows? Medicine advances all the time. There might now be some remedy for your injuries that would allow you to carry a child to term. And if there isn't . . . there are a lot of kids out there who need love and a home."

He paused, studying her face. "So, tell me straight. Do you want to continue—or not?"

Continue, let her feelings deepen, risk loss and pain again?

Did she want to live, or just exist?

After struggling for another minute between fear and desire, she whispered, "I'd . . . like to continue."

"Hallelujah," he murmured, pulling her into his arms. "So, what are the guidelines? You know I love to touch you, but I don't want to force anything or make you uncomfortable."

"Or tempted?"

He grinned. "I'm not sure I want to avoid 'tempted.'"

She paused, a little light-headed after the emotional release of her tears. All of this was so new she'd had no time to think about what she really wanted—or would be comfortable with. "I'd like to continue going places with you. Having you come here to cook. I'd really like to kiss you again, but I'm not sure I can control my reactions if I do."

"How about if I promise not to let you take advantage of me?" he offered with a grin.

"Your control is that good?"

"I would never do anything to hurt a lady," he said, sobering instantly. "No matter how hard it might be to resist. Whatever you are comfortable giving—however little or much—will be enough. I'm just . . . grateful that you're willing to give us another chance. And determined to prevent any future . . . 'couch disasters.'"

"We're agreed, then?"

He nodded.

"So . . . I can kiss you good night?"

"As long as it's not 'goodbye.'"

She went up on tiptoe and kissed him gently on the lips, savoring his closeness. Her body clamored for more, but her mind, relishing this unthreatening, incredibly comforting contact, ignored it. He stayed absolutely still, letting her kiss him, but not trying to deepen or prolong it.

"So . . . that's okay with you?" she whispered as she broke the kiss.

"More than okay. Wonderful. You have permission to repeat it as often as you like."

"Thank you, Brice McAllister. For being the man you

are."

"Just for you, sweetheart."

Tentatively, he put his arm around her, and she let him, walking with him to the door. Standing on the threshold, he kissed her cheek. "Good night, Mary. Thanks again for a wonderful day."

"Good night, Brice. Thanks for understanding—and for making me want to truly live again."

He put on his hat, tipped it to her and walked to his truck, then gave her a wave before driving off. Pensive, she drifted back into the living room to drop down onto the "disaster" couch.

And smiled sadly. Painful as it was to tell him what had happened, she felt . . . a sort of healing calm. As if an old bandage had been ripped off, exposing the still-raw wound to healing air. The hurt was still there—would always be there.

But for the first time in a long time, she was no longer carrying the burden of it alone. For the first time since the shooting, she caught glimmers of a future that didn't leave her alone forever.

THREE WEEKS LATER, Mary sat in her kitchen, brewing espresso to put in the carafe they'd take with them on her excursion with Brice.

Since the night she'd dissolved into tears and confessed

some of her history, she'd seen him once or twice a week. Sometimes cooking with Bunny at the house, sometimes going to events in town or festivals in San Antonio or Austin.

She'd even visited his condo—a cold, sterile white box furnished in a minimalist, ultramodern style that she told him reminded her of the anteroom of a modern art gallery. He'd confessed with chagrin that, busy with training after he'd first joined the Rangers, he'd let a girlfriend decorate it. Unfortunately, the furnishings had lasted longer than the relationship. He'd never felt at home there, but being on the road as much as he was, he hadn't taken the time to change it.

It might, he suggested, be a future project they could take on together.

So he seemed to believe in a future. Maybe she should take his suggestion and make an appointment with the specialist she'd found at the Medical Center in Houston, have them do a new workup and see if there were in fact treatments now that would offer her the chance to bear a healthy child. An ability that would free her to give herself to him completely, and if they decided to make their union permanent, give him the children that a man who loved them so much deserved.

The notion was so painfully precious she couldn't let herself hope for it.

Brice continued to be the same compassionate, understanding man who'd gradually weaned her out of wariness.

He let her kiss him, kissed her back, took advantage of every opportunity to touch her hand, stroke her back, or give her a hug.

Part of her felt bad that she'd made him keep his desire on such a short leash. There were ways she could satisfy him, of course, without risking pregnancy, but she wasn't quite ready—yet—to try something that might strain both their controls past the breaking point.

Better to know for sure where the relationship was going before committing to something that, if it turned out to be a mistake, would be irrecoverable.

Even with the reservations about the physical restraints, she felt more complete, happier, than she had since the carefree days before the shooting. More aware every day of how much, these last three years, she'd been merely existing. Learning again how opening herself to affection and involvement could brighten and bring joy.

Brice continued to look for events and entertainments he thought she'd enjoy. Which was why, this early Saturday, he would be arriving soon to take her to a plant nursery Abby had discovered that specialized in vegetables, perennials, and shrubs that grew well in the Hill Country area.

Having already killed her share of some of her favorite plants that her *nonna* had grown in California, she was looking forward to choosing some that might thrive rather than wither before her eyes.

Hearing the sound of a truck engine, she hopped up to

greet Brice at the door. He walked in, so big and masterful and delicious, picked her up and swung her around, then gave her an exaggerated kiss on the lips. "How's my best girl?"

"Pert as a cricket," she said, using another of the Texas-isms he'd taught her.

He laughed. "Let's load up the coffee—and dare I hope there are biscotti to go with it?"

"Of course. A gentleman who escorts a lady to one of her favorite places in the world deserves only the best."

"What are your other favorite places in the world? I'm keeping a list," he said with a grin. "Just to give myself options. Libraries, obviously. Bookstores, I would imagine. Antique or junktique shops. Plant nurseries and . . ."

"Good wineries. Fine restaurants. And a certain place with big rocks by a trickling stream, with cattle grazing in a nearby pasture, a soft breeze blowing, the scent of water, wildflowers, meadow grass . . ."

Something in his face changed, going from teasing to more intense. "The Triple A?"

She nodded.

"So you could see . . . maybe living in a cottage there someday?"

"A cottage overlooking that location? Now, that would be heaven." And it would. All that natural beauty, shared with a man who was even more amazing.

"I'll keep it in mind. Now we better be off. We promised

Bunny she could come cook dinner with us tonight."

"Yes, I need to redeem myself. I think she's jealous that I've had you all to myself on several trips. Even though she agreed that she'd be bored going to wineries and the concert in Austin was past her bedtime."

"She wouldn't stay mad at you. Besides, I'm sure Elaine has emphasized that adults do adult things sometimes, like she and Tom do."

"I just have to woo her back by fixing her favorite things tonight."

"Anything you cook is my favorite, so that's easy to agree with."

They walked to the truck, where he took her hand to help her up and gave her another long, lingering kiss.

"What was that for?" she asked dreamily after he released her.

"Just because. It's a beautiful day, I'm taking my favorite lady to one of her favorite places in the world. With espresso and biscotti. What could be better?"

IT TOOK THEM about an hour to reach the nursery, which was located along a back road between Fredericksburg and Johnson City.

Walking in, Mary was delighted to discover the business featured a number of display gardens that, although it was heading into fall, still boasted a wealth of flowering plants.

"Why don't we wander around for a bit and then you can talk to a staff person about what you've seen that you like?" Brice suggested.

"Sounds like a plan!"

Brice trailing indulgently behind her, she walked slowly past dry rock gardens with a wide array of succulents in various shapes and sizes, a hillside of grasses of different heights and colors, then a long bed that featured a planting of crepe myrtle trees, deep pink, then ruby, then lavender, their peeling, cinnamon-striped bark accenting the large sprays of flowers. Planted at their feet were a variety of lantanas, white-flowered under the pink trees, orange-and-red under the ruby, yellow under the lavender. Another bed held a sprawl of starry purple asters in full bloom beside the deep lavender spikes of gayflowers.

"This is wonderful!" she said, exuberant with delight as she looked back at Brice. "I want some of everything!"

"I don't think I can fit all that in the truck," he said with a straight face. "Maybe we better find an employee and start narrowing down the list."

He hailed a garden specialist, who asked what color flowers she preferred and what the planting locations offered in terms of soil and moisture level. In addition to the asters and gayflower, she added some Carolina jasmine for winter bloom, an old-fashioned flowering quince for early spring bloom, and a winter honeysuckle, as well as several pots of

Texas tarragon to add to her herb bed.

Once she'd lined up her purchases, they took their coffee and biscotti to a picnic area on the grounds. "It is so beautiful here!" she told him as she poured his coffee. "Someday I want my garden to look like that," she gestured toward the display garden. "Thanks for indulging me. I just hope you weren't too bored."

"I like flowers. I just don't like weeding or tending them. Besides, it makes me happy to see you happy."

"That sentiment deserves a kiss," she said, suiting action to her words. "I like making you happy too," she added after breaking the kiss.

"Then just keep being you." The sincerity of the look he gave her, the tenderness in his face, made her feel like melting inside. Her resistance to letting anyone close again had been rock solid when they first met. But little by little, he'd chipped away at it, until she felt, with more remarks like that, the whole structure was in imminent danger of collapse.

Maybe it was time to schedule that appointment with the Houston specialist and make an informed choice on one option or the other. The possibility of a safe pregnancy, or permanent safety from pregnancy. Because Brice's control might be as solid at Hill Country granite, but more and more, she was longing to do away with restraint and give herself completely to the man with whom, she admitted to herself, if not yet to him, she was falling in love with.

Hands entwined, they walked back to the truck. "We'll

have just enough time after we get home to get these into the ground before Bunny comes over," he said as he helped her stow the plants into the back of his truck.

"I thought you didn't like planting and tending."

"Only for you, sweetheart. Besides, I need the space back."

Chuckling, she let him help her into the cab chatting on the way back about the new plants and where in the garden she planned to put them. Brice told her the case he'd been working was almost ready to close, although of course he couldn't give her any details. Not that, resisting as always that aspect of his life, she would have asked for any.

When he pulled the vehicle into her driveway, she shifted to hop out. He put a hand on her wrist to restrain her.

She looked up, smiling. "What? Another kiss?" She made an exaggerated pucker and closed her eyes.

He kissed her lightly, but when she opened her eyes, he was wearing an intense expression. "I think sometime soon we need to have a serious talk about the future. If you think you might be anywhere near ready."

A flutter of nervousness and excitement swirled in her belly. She didn't pretend to misunderstand what he was asking. Was she ready?

"Give me a day or so to consider my answer."

She felt a pang at the look of disappointment that briefly crossed his face before he nodded. "Fair enough."

If she had disappointed him, he gave no more evidence

of it, teasing her again by groaning at the supposedly excessive weight of the shrubs she'd bought and the vast number of holes they'd have to dig to get all the plants in the ground and watered in.

By the time they had the truck unloaded and the plants prepped, Bunny was calling a hello.

After the stint in the garden, in which Bunny participated enthusiastically, they spent the evening fixing and eating dinner—Bunny's favorite chicken she got to pound—playing games and amusing the little girl, with no further private discussion. Brice didn't mention the prospect again before kissing her goodbye and carrying a tired-out Bunny back home.

She stood by the back door, watching him until he disappeared inside the Edgertons' house with his sleepy burden. Was she ready to move on, really move on? Take the risk of making a commitment to him—if he did in fact intend to propose?

She didn't think, knowing her history and his deep sense of responsibility, he'd want to talk about a commitment less formal than marriage. He wouldn't ask her to make the potentially heartbreaking choice of ending for good all chance of bearing a child unless he was prepared to make their relationship officially permanent.

A life with Brice at her side—teasing, watching, guarding, loving her. Wonderful. Even more wonderful, being able to give passion free rein, explore his body and let him explore hers as she'd longed to do now for what seemed forever.

She still felt strongly that a man like Brice needed to be able to have children of his own. Before she gave him her answer, she would consult that specialist in Houston.

Chapter Twelve

THE MIDDLE OF the next week, Brice drove into Whiskey River to talk with Tom at the bank. As usual, while he drove along, his thoughts cycled back to Mary.

How close they'd come to breaking up, before she revealed a story of loss more poignant and tragic than anything he could have imagined.

No wonder she wasn't too enamored of the police if, after that terrible crime, the perpetrators had never been found. A lawman's primary job was to get dangerous criminals off the streets, so they couldn't endanger peaceful citizens going about their everyday lives. She'd have a lot of justification for believing if they couldn't do that, what good were they?

The incident itself was disturbing enough, but to know that it had happened to a woman who loved children and was as good with them as Mary made his chest ache. He'd not been able to prevent himself from going to hold her while she wept, anguished for her loss, feeling helpless at knowing there was nothing he could ever do to make that right.

After learning the true depth of that darkness in her past, he understood much better why she had locked herself away from living, putting up a boundary wall of silence, masking her attractiveness so no one would be tempted to breach it.

No one until him. He felt humbled and honored that she'd trusted him enough to want to finally emerge from the shadows.

If he hadn't already been in love with her, knowing what she'd survived and the courage it had taken not to let it permanently scar her life would have pushed him over the edge.

Course, the fact that she was gorgeous and cooked like a top chef didn't hurt, he thought, smiling.

By now, he was approaching the outskirts of Whiskey River. He slowed the truck to the municipal speed limit, and a few minutes later, pulled into the bank parking lot.

He could, of course, have spoken to his friend over the weekend, but since this involved official business, he preferred to conduct the interview in uniform and at work.

He and his team had managed to track most of the spurious deposits and were very near to closing in on the prime suspect they'd been watching now for nearly two months. The man had arranged transfers to straw accounts in banks in a scattering of small towns, with no geographic pattern, which had made it harder to center in on where he was operating from. If there had been any recent suspicious transfers into the Whiskey River bank, Brice could add one more clue to help them close the net.

Hoping he'd get that clue, he walked in, nodding to the tellers and employees in the outer office, all of whom knew him and called a greeting. After exchanging a few words with Tom's secretary, he was ushered into his friend's office.

"Badged up and in uniform!" Tom eyed him up and down. "I'm guessing this isn't a social call?"

"Investigative business this time."

"What can I help you with?"

"Has the bank gotten any demand drafts from any San Antonio banks payable to someone with a recently opened account?"

"I'll check, but we don't deal much with demand drafts. Most of our business is in mortgages and small business loans. Let me call Larry Franklin, our CFO." He picked up the phone and made a short call. "Let's go into Larry's office. He knows the records programs better than I do and can check faster."

Brice followed his friend into another office, where a tall man whom he'd hadn't met before rose to shake his hand. After an exchange of greetings, the financial analyst logged into a series of programs, turning back to Brice a few minutes later. "No, we haven't done any demand drafts for more than six months. Do you need me to go back farther than that?"

"No, anything connected to what we're working on would have been recent."

"Some sort of bank fraud, I'm guessing."

Brice merely nodded, not being at liberty to give them any details. "Thanks for your help."

Not surprised, but a little disappointed, he walked back with Tom to his office. Bullies had always angered him, and he looked on those who committed financial fraud as just another kind of bully. Rather than earn money legitimately, they stole from others, justifying it by saying, "the rich can afford it."

Unfortunately, though the rich might be able to afford it, all too often salaried bank officials and small-time investors got caught up as collateral damage in their schemes, losing their jobs or their money for not catching on to the fraud.

He couldn't wait to get the final piece of evidence that would guarantee a successful prosecution and send the current perpetrator to prison.

"Have time for lunch?" Tom asked.

"I'm supposed to meet Mary on her lunch hour," Brice said. "We don't normally meet during business hours, so it must be important and I don't want to miss it."

"Getting kinda hot and heavy there, aren't you?" Tom asked.

"Things are progressing," Brice said noncommittally. The last thing he wanted was Mary's neighbor teasing her about their involvement—putting her on the spot to either confirm or deny a relationship. "But nothing official. So please don't say anything to anyone—especially not to

Bunny."

"She'd be over the moon if her two favorite people got hitched." Tom laughed and slapped his desk. "Hot damn! Girls all over Texas should be weeping tonight. I think this Texas Ranger has taken himself off the market."

Frowning, Brice held up a hand. "Don't be planning the bachelor party yet. You know how wary Mary is. If she thinks she's being pressured to make a choice, she may back away."

"Back away before you get her lassoed for good?" Tom said, grinning. "Okay, I'll keep it under my hat, but I couldn't be more pleased. For both of you."

"Yeah, well, it's hardly a done deal yet, for either of us, so zip-lip on this."

Tom sobered. "If there is a chance you two might get together, I wouldn't want to do anything to jeopardize that. She's a sweet girl, and I can't think of anyone who would deserve her more than you. Before you go, though, there's one other thing."

On the point of turning to go out, Brice halted. "What's on your mind?"

Tom motioned him to a chair and curious, Brice sat down. "I'm glad you came in today. I was debating calling you about this, but technically, it's an ethically questionable area. I got the info in confidence, and privacy issues should prohibit me from saying anything. But since it involves your brothers and the Triple A, I thought I should let you know."

"What about the Triple A?"

"As I'm sure you know, Duncan and Grant applied for a small business loan to do the renovations on the Scott barn, to turn it into a venue that could be used to host events for kids, veterans, agricultural meetings and so forth."

"Yes. Go on."

"Rich, who handles small business loans for us, let slip to me yesterday that he was really conflicted about the progress of the loan. He'd been about to approve it at the usual rate when one of the board of directors came into his office and told him he didn't think the application qualified under the most-favored rates. That since the ranch had been around for a long time and was a large business, it should be charged a higher corporate rate. Brice, the repayment period on that type of loan is short and the interest rate would significantly increase the monthly payment. Rich didn't want to issue the loan under those terms, but the board member made it clear that he would be watching, and if Rich valued his position at the bank, he better make the loan on the terms the member suggested."

Duncan was going to be furious, and Grant would probably want to take the loan officer apart limb from limb. "Did he tell you who the board member was?"

"Not outright, but I can probably guess. Knowing the bad blood between your brother and Marshal Thomason, I'd guess that it was Carl Wagner—who, you may remember, is the brother-in-law of Henry Thomason, Marshall's father.

Fair or not, the Thomasons still wield a lot of power around this town. I can see why Rich is so torn over this."

As angry as he knew his brothers were going to be, Brice jumped up, pacing the room as he thought rapidly. "What happens next in the loan process?"

"Rich will call your brothers in to look at the terms of the loan, which they can then either accept or reject."

"Has that meeting been set up yet?"

"I'm not sure. But it should be soon."

"I'd better go talk to them right away, then."

"I would. Oh, and one more thing. Elaine said in one of her yoga classes some of the bigwig ladies in town attend, that Melissa Thomason, Marshall's mother, was talking about how his latest project would bring an exotic hunting ranch to the area. How good it would be for business, more tourists coming into the restaurants, bars, and shops."

A hunting ranch for exotic animals? The words of one of the ranchers he'd questioned in the Diner came suddenly back. *Why deal with animals that are hardly worth spit in a good year? Said he'd stock something better than that.*

Brice felt like slapping himself on the forehead for not having thought of that possibility. Big-game ranches had sprung up in several areas of the Hill Country and West Texas. Originally stocked by excess animals sold by zoos, the ranches obtained expensive trophy fees from hunters who wanted an African safari experience right at home in Texas.

To be fair, some of the ranches didn't permit hunting

and acted instead as wildlife refuges dedicated to building up stock of rare and endangered species, often exporting some of the animals back to their native lands where their numbers had been depleted.

Those that did sponsor hunts, though, made lots of money. In addition to their hefty charges for lodging, meals and hunting guides, he'd heard the trophy fee for a guest successfully bagging even one of the more common animals, like an oryx, started at about four hundred dollars. For something more rare, like sitatunga antelope or a black wildebeest, the fee could run as high as fifteen thousand dollars.

He looked up to see Tom watching him soberly.

"Exotic animal hunting ranch. Yes, that would make sense. Nothing for him to do but buy the animals, hire a manager, and rake in the profits."

"Triple A land would be a prize addition. All those hills for ibex and antelope to climb, a long river border with natural water, hundreds of acres in pristine condition. Sorry, Brice. Hope you can work something out."

"Thanks for letting me know, Tom. I'll tell my brothers not to let on that they knew the terms had been changed before they arrive for that meeting."

"Appreciate it. And no problem—my conscience is mostly clear. Teammates stick together. Especially when the family of one is about to get screwed by a guy who never broke a sweat doing anything useful in his life."

Giving Tom a nod, Brice walked out. He had to be in New Braunfels this afternoon, and he needed to see his brothers before he left town. Regretfully, he was going to have to cancel lunch with Mary. Fortunately, they now knew each other well enough that he didn't think she would take it as a brush-off.

After hopping into this truck, he texted Mary, "*Had something come up about the ranch. Need to see D and G before leaving town so won't have time for lunch. Do dinner later this week?*"

With a grumble of irritation, he sent the text, then another to both his brothers, telling them he needed to meet them at the McAllister ranch house immediately on a matter of great urgency.

Texts sent, he started the truck and headed out to the Triple A.

They might never be able to pin the harassment episodes on Thomason, but this financial maneuvering pretty much proved to Brice that he must have been behind them. Thomason would have known that paying a higher rate on the loan needed to make the improvements that would offset the loss of their herd bull's stud fees would strain the ranch's slender cash reserves to the limit. Maybe, if Thomason was lucky and the price of beef dropped, reduce their income enough to force them once again into having to sell off land or risk foreclosure on loans they no longer had enough cash income to pay.

Time for a strategy session. The McAllisters might not have the money the Thomasons boasted, but their family had been born and bred in these limestone hills for over a hundred and sixty years, and no slimy rich-boy wuss was going to drive them out now.

By the time he reached the ranch house, Grant's vehicle was parked by the door. As Brice climbed out of his truck, his brother walked over to meet him.

"So what was so important that we needed to circle the wagons immediately?" he asked, coming over to give Brice their traditional one-armed brother's hug. Waggling his eyebrows, he added, "Got an important announcement to make about a certain lady? Given how much time you've been spending in Whiskey River lately, I wouldn't be surprised. Since I doubt it's my or Duncan's congenial company that's bringing you . . ."

Looking at what must be the thundercloud expression on Brice's face, Grant let the sentence trail off. "This is something serious, isn't it?"

Brice nodded. "Is Duncan here? I'd rather tell you both at once."

"In the den, having lunch. Harrison's in her office, working on the stud books, trying to see what we could rearrange with the customers who'd been counting on using Halsey this year, see if maybe they would accept one of the other, less-experienced stud bulls. For a lower fee, of course," he added, sighing. "Abby's down at her shop, so we can talk without being interrupted."

Duncan rose as he entered, giving him a hug. "Harrison made some of her mother's famous chili last night. There's plenty, if you'd like to heat a bowl for lunch, and soda water's in the fridge." Unlike Grant, his always-serious older brother didn't make any attempt at a joke.

Anything that touched the ranch was deadly serious to Duncan. Which, given the endless hours of work and worry he'd put into running it over the last decade, Brice understood completely.

After all three brothers were seated, food before them, Brice briefly summarized what Tom had confided to him. "I guess Thomason figured after the income loss the death of Halsey represented, it was time to go for the kill with a financial deal that would break the Triple A," he finished.

Grant jumped up, swearing, but Duncan just held out a hand, motioning him to calm.

"Thanks for calling everyone here, Brice. I was going to try to get us together anyway. I got the notice this morning to meet at the bank tomorrow—in the mail. Strange, I thought, because usually Rich would just call or text me. The notice said something about 'terms of the loan may have been changed to reflect current bank rates.' So I already suspected something was up. But there's more bad news."

"What else?" Grant demanded.

Duncan picked up a piece of paper and held it up. "The property tax bill for the ranch. The assessment of the land value usually goes up a bit every year—funny how it seldom goes down, no matter how bad a year it's been," he added bitterly. "But the bill we just got is significantly, eyebrow-raisingly higher than last year's. In the small print, it said the added evaluation is for the 'capital improvements to the barn, on property formally known as the Scott Ranch.'"

"But those improvements haven't even been made yet!" Grant said angrily.

"Fortunately, I know a little something about property taxes. I never just get the tax bill and pay it until after carefully comparing my year-to-year records to determine what the percentage increase is. Although this significant an increase should have opened any rancher's eyes, even someone with a much larger and more profitable spread who doesn't usually pay too much attention to tax bill details."

"So what can be done?" Grant asked.

"And who makes the assessments?" Brice added.

"Charity Johnson is the county assessment officer. She's young and hasn't been on the job long. I suspect her mortgage, and maybe credit cards, were issued by the same bank where Thomason Senior's brother-in-law is on the board."

"So she, like Rich, could have been subjected to some pressure?" Grant said.

"And most likely from the same source," Brice added. "It all comes back to Thomason."

"Boy, I wish I could rearrange his pretty face," Grant said hotly.

"The assessor might have salved her conscience by knowing anyone who looked closely at the bill could get around it. For one, property can only be assessed for its value on January first of the current year. Well before we were even thinking of converting the barn to other uses. Then the estimate of the assessed value is sent in May. The one we got indicated a slight increase, but nothing on the order of this one," he said, holding up the paper. "If the property were reassessed at a higher value later, the law says we have to get a copy of the reassessment and the reasons for it. We've received nothing. Finally, the property owner has the right to appeal the reassessment to an appraisal board. Which would never uphold a jack-up in value for a future project. She could send this out, getting whoever was pressuring her off her back, knowing that unless we were total idiots, we wouldn't end up having to pay the increase."

"How could she be sure you'd check it closely?" Brice asked, not as charitable as his brother.

Duncan shrugged. "Probably figured if I wasn't smart enough to keep a close eye over my own finances and got screwed, it was my fault."

"So what do we do?" Grant asked. "The property tax can be handled by an appeal of the appraisal, which you say we won't have any trouble winning. What about the loan?"

Duncan blew out a breath. "We'll have to figure something else out about that."

"More satisfying than rearranging Marshall's pretty face

would be torpedoing his deal," Brice said.

"I don't know," Grant said. "Right now, the idea of rearranging his pretty face is awfully appealing."

"So how do we call off the bank?" Brice asked.

"Aside from putting out a hit on the double-dealing board member? I hear we know a Texas Ranger sharpshooter." Grant sighed. "That's only partly a joke."

"Better to have all the responsible parties present and accounted for, so they get to witness the destruction of their plans. Okay, Thomason and his clique have exercised a lot of influence in this town for a long time. Only the Kellys probably have more pull—though fortunately, they remember where they came from and would never play a dirty trick on a fellow rancher. Maybe it's time we harnessed the power of all the 'little guys.'"

Brice looked up, a surge of excitement replacing his anger. "I think I know where you're headed with this. You were recently elected president of the local Cattleman's Association, weren't you?"

Duncan nodded. "Let me make some phone calls. Then, when we go into that meeting tomorrow, we'll be locked and loaded."

"What's your plan, bro?" Grant asked.

"We'll talk with Rich first. This might be much ado about nothing. But if he has been pressured to change the loan terms, we go straight to the bank president. Tell him that our family has been doing business with his bank for three generations, but if he supports the board member in changing the loan terms, we will take our loan application, and all our other banking business, somewhere else, permanently. Not only us, but every other rancher in the association."

"When you make that call to the other members, you might also tell them about Marshall's underhanded dealings. Tell them it might be better for Whiskey River's reputation as a town where honest, hardworking people live if they use a different firm, any other firm, for any future real estate transactions."

"Good idea. If Thomason goes through with his plan to put an exotic animal hunting ranch on the lowland property he's already bought, there isn't much we can do."

"I don't know," Grant said with a slow smile. "I understand they require miles of high fencing, and we all know how vulnerable to damage fences are."

"If it wouldn't put us on his level, I'd be tempted," Duncan admitted. "So, are we in agreement?"

"Absolutely," Grant said.

"I have to go to San Marcos this afternoon, but I could come back tomorrow and make that meeting with you, if you want," Brice offered, still simmering mad and almost looking forward to a confrontation.

"Thanks, little brother, but you don't need to rearrange your schedule. I think Grant and I can handle it. But we're indebted to you for keeping your ear to the ground and finally flushing out what Thomason's true intentions were. We might never be able to nail him for the damage those incidents caused the ranch, but putting a spike in the wheel of his business dealings will still be totally satisfying."

"You're that sure the other ranchers will back us up?" Grant asked.

Duncan gave him a look. "Can you name me anyone who grew up around here—other than his townie friends—who likes or trusts the guy?"

"Good point."

After a glance at the clock, Brice said, "I'd better head off to New Braunfels. Have to meet a court official."

"Any closer to bringing that current case to a close?" Duncan asked.

Brice held up his thumb and forefinger about a millimeter apart. "This close. And after tracking him for months, it's going to be so satisfying to put this guy away."

"Score another one for the good guys," Grant said, slapping him on the shoulder. "Go get 'em, Texas Ranger."

BACK IN HIS truck, driving out toward the main road to New Braunfels, Brice heard a text ping. Figuring it was Mary, he pulled over.

Canceling lunch no problem. May have to go out of town for a few days, library business, which was what I was going to tell you. Text you when I get back. She ended it with some "kiss" emojis.

Brice felt a pang of disappointment. He hated that he'd missed her. He'd been looking forward to seeing her again today or tomorrow. Now he would have to wait.

Irritation over that fact made him even more determined to catch the slimeball who was bilking banks.

Chapter Thirteen

THREE DAYS LATER, Mary drove back toward Whiskey River. After calling the specialist's office and finding that due to a cancellation, there was an appointment available the following day, she'd asked Shirley for time off, which was granted without her needing to provide any explanation. Shirley said if she needed time, she was welcome to it, so she snapped up the vacant slot.

She'd planned to tell Brice at their lunch why she was going out of town, but when he had to cancel, decided she didn't want to convey that news in a text or phone call. Better to see him face-to-face since, for better or worse, he was the one whose advice had spurred her to finally take this step.

She'd overnighted in a hotel near the medical center, spent a full day doing routine testing and then having the consultation, another night in the hotel, and driven back today.

Although the specialist had advised her they would need to schedule more specific tests, she'd also provided a ray of hope that there might now be treatments that would allow her, if she could get pregnant, to carry the child to term.

Such brilliant, wonderful, exciting news also needed to be delivered in person. As soon as she got back home, she'd text Brice and see when he'd be in town next.

She was pretty sure she'd be ready to have that serious talk about their future.

It was midafternoon when she pulled into her driveway, the sight of her little cottage always raising her spirits. Maybe she'd ask Brice to come for dinner, use some of the tomato sauce she'd frozen and make fresh spaghetti noodles for him, accompanied by one of the Super Texan wines she'd bought on their Oktoberfest trip. Make it a special evening worthy of a new beginning.

Humming, she pulled her overnight bag out of the car and walked to the door, mentally going over a grocery shopping list in her mind as she unlocked it and backed in, pulling the bag behind her. Then turned around and stopped cold.

"Joey!" she gasped. "What are you doing here?"

The intruder gave her the charming smile that had gotten him out of trouble so many times. "Hey, sis, aren't you going to give your baby brother a hug?"

Conflicting emotions pulled at her. He was her brother, and despite what had happened, she still loved him, even if she didn't want to be around him anymore. Reluctantly, she walked over to give him the hug he requested.

"Okay, we've hugged," she said, stepping away. "I won't

bother asking how you got in, since you've been able to pick any lock ever made since you were twelve." Suddenly concerned about who might have seen him, she said, "When did you get here?"

"This afternoon. Don't worry, nobody saw me come in. I'm not stupid, right?"

Mary refrained from answering that question. "So what are you doing here? No, wait—don't tell me. You're in some kind of trouble, aren't you?"

"Now, why do you always think that? Couldn't I just want to catch up with my big sister? I've missed you since you moved away. You know how sorry I was about . . . everything."

"Sorry you lent us your car after messing up a deal that had Brokavich's hoods out looking to teach Sal Giordano's nephew a lesson?" she said bitterly. "Sorry I lost the man I loved and my child?"

"Jeez, sis, you know I am. And you know Uncle Sal promised he'd find the punks and take care of them."

"That won't bring back Ian. Okay, enough old history. Tell me why you're really here."

He continued grinning at her, and immediately suspicious, she leaned closer. Her heart sank. Sure enough, his pupils were dilated. He was using again.

"You can't stay here, Joey. Whatever you're running from, if you knew where to find me, they will too. In fact, the house of an out-of-town relative is the first place someone would look. Couldn't Uncle Sal take care of whatever made you run?"

"Well, there was a little problem with Uncle Sal over some . . . you know, merchandise."

"Don't tell me you were snitching some of his supply. Joey!"

He waved a hand. "Don't worry, we'll be cool again soon. I just needed to blow town for a while until he simmers down. And there are a few people I'd rather not meet right now."

"If someone is after you, you definitely can't stay here. I love you, but I told you long ago if you wouldn't give up being a bag handler for Uncle Sal, I couldn't continue to see you. You chose that life, Joey. Papa and I chose to walk away. Whatever your situation is, you'll have to resolve it on your own. I've already been collateral damage to your problems once, and I refuse to do that again."

Besides which, Bunny might come over at any time. She'd not allow her wayward brother to put that precious child in danger. Realizing that it was getting dark and she'd need to turn on lights soon, she hurried to the windows facing the yard—windows the Edgertons might be able to see through—and lowered all the blinds.

"Okay, okay. So I can spend the night, right? Maybe I'll move on tomorrow, go see the old man in Florida."

"You will absolutely not go see Papa," she said furiously. "What happened devastated him too. He's made a new life for himself, even found a lovely lady who's helped him through his grief over losing Mama. I promise you, if I find out you've left here and gone to Papa's, I'll call the cops on you myself."

"Jeez, you're such a straight arrow now for someone who used to be Uncle Sal's little darling."

"Not after I got old enough to realize what was going on. You were the one fascinated by his world. I never was."

"He let you go, didn't he? Even though it broke his heart."

Mary refused to feel guilty about that. "I'm sure he got over it."

"I'm not so sure. Family is family, Maria."

"Which is the only reason I don't throw you out on your ear here and now! But by heaven, if you aren't gone by tomorrow night, I swear I will. Just in case someone does come looking, I don't want to know where you go."

"Okay, okay, I'll think about it. Now, why don't you calm down, pour some wine and make us something to eat? It's almost dinnertime."

Anything she fixed would taste like sawdust until she got rid of her brother, but cooking would take her mind off her anger and panic. But what if Bunny tried to come over?

She grabbed the handbag she'd dropped on the floor and extracted her phone, quickly typing Elaine a text saying she was feeling under the weather, so it would be better to keep Bunny at home for now and that she'd text again when she felt better. Fingers trembling, she hit "send."

Elaine would probably text back, asking if she could bring something over or do anything, but after Mary thanked her and turned down the offer, she wouldn't intrude.

Thank heaven Brice was working on his case out of town this week.

She had to make sure Joey was gone before Brice got back.

IT WAS FAIRLY late when Brice drove back into Whiskey River, but with the final piece of evidence gathered and the raid to capture the culprit set up, he was in a mood to celebrate. And there wasn't anyone he'd rather celebrate with than Mary. Plus, he was curious about her sudden trip. As reclusive as she'd been since arriving in Whiskey River, he couldn't see her volunteering to go out of town on assignment for the library.

And what would a library need her to go out of town for?

Maybe he could propose some outrageous possibilities, just to see her laugh, he thought, smiling at the thought.

He'd intended to drive straight out to the Scott ranch house to spend the night. But the town of Whiskey River was on the way . . . . He could drive past Mary's cottage, see if the lights were still on. If so, maybe beg a cup of espresso and one of her delicious cookies to keep him from getting sleepy on his drive out to the ranch.

And maybe claim a few of her even more delicious kisses.

Yes, he'd definitely drive by the house.

Ten minutes later, he eased his truck to a stop near her door. Sure enough, he saw lights on behind the drawn curtains. Hoping he wouldn't surprise her getting ready for bed in a silky nightgown—a man's ability to resist temptation only stretched so far—he knocked on the door.

He waited, but there was no answer. Maybe she was getting ready for bed. Disappointed, he was about to turn to go when he noticed the front door was shut, but not fully closed. Sure enough, when he turned the knob, the door opened easily.

Concern for her safety immediately ratcheting up, he decided he'd creep in quietly, so as not to disturb her if she was showering or changing into her nightgown, make sure things looked okay, and turn the button knob so the door would at least lock behind him. Then text her from his truck to let her know she needed to turn the dead bolt, and he wasn't driving away until she'd done so and texted him back.

But as he slipped in, he saw her emerge from the hallway to the bedrooms—followed by a dark-haired man who had his hand on her shoulder.

He froze, confused, his mind racing. When she'd told him about the death of her fiancé and child, a very understandable reason for wanting to start life over somewhere else, he'd stopped worrying that she might be hiding from an abusive ex. So who was this man? Someone else from her past who menaced her?

Or was he seeing something entirely different?

Unbidden, the memory of the misdirected text from Ashley, setting up a rendezvous with another man while he was away, flashed back into his head.

Before he could decide what to say or do, the man saw him and halted, muttering an expletive that made Mary's gaze swivel in his direction.

"Brice?" she whispered, putting a hand to her throat as her eyes widened in surprise. "I . . . I didn't think you'd be back until later this week."

His gaze went from her to the visitor and back. "So I can see."

He waited for an explanation, but none was forthcoming. Mary looked—upset, but he didn't get any sense that she felt threatened, or was being held against her will.

Maybe it was the other possibility. Feeling like he'd just been punched in the gut, he said, "I'll just go on back out."

But as he spoke, the tall, dark-haired man walked toward him, a menacing expression on his face. "Who are you to come busting into my sister's house?"

Mary gave him a weak smile. "Brice, meet my little brother, Joey."

With a swagger, her brother walked toward him, a smirk on his face as he looked Brice up and down. His gaze stopped dead when it met the Ranger's star on Brice's chest. "A *Texas Ranger*? You gotta be kidding me!" he said, laughing.

"Maybe Uncle Sal will toss me out of the family," she said dryly. "Joey . . . is paying me an unexpected visit. He'll probably be leaving tomorrow. I expected he would be gone before you got back."

Brice nodded slowly, his brain scrambling to recover from the shock of seeing another man in her house, relief that he was a brother rather than an abusive ex or a secret boyfriend, and trying to process the unspoken dynamics at work.

The brother appeared a little slack-limbed, his eyes blinking rapidly. Brice thought he might be on some sort of drugs. And Mary was clearly unhappy with her brother's presence in her house.

Druggies could be unpredictable. No way was he leaving Mary alone with someone who might hurt her. "Are you okay with him staying here?"

"Just a short visit, *Ranger*. Family matters," her brother answered.

"I asked your sister. Mary?"

The brother laughed again. "Mary? Is that what they call you here? You really did want to leave all of us behind, didn't you, Maria Giordano?"

Maria Giordano? Another shock went through him. So she had changed her name.

"I'll be okay, Brice. Joey's no danger to me."

"She's probably more in danger from you," her brother said. "I don't take to lawmen harassing my sister, see? Or creeping into her house uninvited. I think you need to scram, or she might need to call the cops. Oh—whoops. You are the cops, aren't you?" he said, laughing again.

The guy really was loopy. "Can I talk with you for a minute?" Brice asked her urgently. "Out in my truck."

Mary glanced from Brice to her brother and back, looking upset and conflicted. All his instincts told him she wasn't comfortable with her brother's visit, yet she couldn't bring herself to send him away.

"Sure, go have a little chat with your *boyfriend*," Joey said. "I can spare you for a few minutes. Just remember who's family and who's not."

"As if I could ever forget," she said bitterly.

Silently, she followed Brice out to his truck. Once she'd climbed in, he said, "Now that you can speak freely—is your brother a danger to you?"

"No. I don't think so."

"Is he using something?"

She sighed. "Probably."

"Is he in trouble?"

She nodded. "I told him he could stay the night. And I texted Elaine saying I was sick and for Bunny to stay home until I texted her I was better, so there's no chance of her popping over. I'll . . . I'll try to get him out of the house tomorrow."

"He's part of the past you wanted to get away from." Then something of what she'd told him clicked, and he said, "The car. The one your fiancé was driving when the hit men shot you. It was his car, right? They were gunning for him."

She sighed. "Maybe I better tell you exactly who you were thinking of becoming involved with. You'll probably think again."

"Try me," Brice said, troubled, wondering if all his instincts about her could have been wrong.

"My uncle Sal is head of a small criminal operation in the suburbs of L.A. Gambling, money laundering, high-priced call girls. He has several sons but no daughters, so when I was little, I was his princess. I loved going to his restaurant where he'd show me off and feed me my favorite foods." She laughed without humor. "I'd always noticed the pretty ladies in lovely clothes and perfect makeup who'd come to the restaurant, always leaving with different men, but I was probably ten or eleven before I figured out what was going on. After that, I wanted nothing to do with Uncle Sal. But Joey . . . Joey was always fascinated by the action, the glamour, the money. Papa, who loved his brother, but refused to have anything to do with his activities, tried to dissuade Joey from being drawn in. I did too."

"But he didn't want to hear it," Brice said.

"No. After I learned what was going on, I asked Papa why he didn't move away. He said that family was family, even if he couldn't approve—or change—what they were involved in. Even though he suffered for it. He was an accountant, and although everyone on the street knew he was clean, the police never stopped believing that somehow he must be involved in Uncle Sal's operations. After the shooting, he spent hours by my hospital bed. The first thing I remember when I regained consciousness was Papa holding my hand, crying, and begging my forgiveness for not having moved our family away. It was only later that I learned Ian was dead, my baby was dead, and the shock of the ambush caused my mother to suffer a heart attack she didn't survive. He vowed that day to sever all ties with the family and move away."

"A little too late. Did he?"

She nodded. "He closed his business and moved to Florida. We talk often on the phone, and last year he met a lovely woman to fill the void left by my mother's death. They're married now, and I'm happy for them."

"You changed your name after the shooting?"

"Yes. I wanted a clean slate. People still saw me as 'Uncle Sal's princess,' even after I stopped going to see him. I wanted to be someone different." She blew out a breath. "But I didn't keep my new location secret, which is why Joey knew where to find me. I still get cards from my cousins and phone them sometimes. The women in the family, the ones whose men are involved in the organization, look the other way. I love my aunts and cousins and their children, but I simply couldn't do that anymore." She looked away, her eyes sad. "Now you know all my ugly little secrets."

"We can't help who our family is. We can only choose who we want to be. It took a lot of courage to make that choice, break away from the familiar, head out on your own."

She looked back at him, a mingling of hope and distress. "Does that mean you'll risk tarnishing your stellar Ranger reputation by associating with the likes of me?"

"Unless there are more dark secrets you haven't revealed, I don't see that you've done anything to have less than a stellar reputation yourself. So how could yours tarnish mine?"

"Do you mean that?"

"Sweetheart, you know I always say what I mean." Then, she looked so vulnerable and fragile, he had to pull her into his arms. "It'll be okay. Are you sure you don't want me to take your brother and drop him over the state line somewhere?"

"No. I'll talk to him. Make sure he leaves sometime tomorrow."

"How are you going to convince him of that? If he feels safe laying low here, he's going to resist having to go somewhere else."

"I don't know," she admitted. "But I'll think of something. Now, I better get back."

He continued to hold her, placing a kiss on her forehead.

"It goes against everything in me to let you go back in that house with him. Sure I can't sleep on your couch? I'd feel a lot better if I were close enough to protect you."

"I promise, Brice, Joey is no danger to me. It would just cause problems if you tried to stay over. I don't want to argue with him. One way or another, I'll get him to leave tomorrow."

"Okay. But I will be checking tomorrow to see that he's gone. And you can tell him that. Will you go to work as usual?"

"Yes. I'll want him to be gone by the time I get home, and I don't want to see him leave or know where he goes."

"If anything happens to make you feel threatened or even uncomfortable, call or text me immediately. Promise?"

"I promise." Before she slipped out of the truck, she kissed him, a fervent, passionate, all-in kiss that sent his pulse rate soaring. "I'll see you tomorrow, then."

"Count on it."

Still not happy with the situation, he watched her walk back to the house, giving him a little wave from the front door. Much as he'd like to, he couldn't override her wishes and insist on staying in the house.

But he sure as heck was going to spend the night parked right outside her door, where he could get to her in a minute if she were in trouble. It wouldn't be the first time he'd slept in his truck on a stakeout.

He never expected to be doing it to protect the woman

with whom he'd fallen in love with.

The woman he loved. Maria Giordano, niece of a small-time L.A. criminal. He shook his head wryly. Her brother had probably been justified in laughing out loud.

CRAMPED FROM THE uncomfortable sleeping position and hungry, Brice woke as early morning light crept through his windshield. Judging by the sun, Mary—Maria—should be up, getting ready for work. Wishing he had a cup of coffee, Brice grabbed his phone and texted, *Everything okay?*

A few minutes later, she texted back, *Everything's fine. Having breakfast before work.*

Good, he replied. *See you this afternoon.*

But he actually saw her sooner, for when she walked out to get into her car, she spotted him in his truck. Stopping short, she shook her head, then walked over to the driver's side of the truck while he lowered the window.

"You stayed outside all night, didn't you?"

He shrugged. "The ranch would be too far away if something had happened."

She blew him a kiss. "That was terribly sweet, if unnecessary. I owe you a breakfast and some strong coffee. I'd do the coffee now, but I need to get to work."

"Did your brother agree to leave today?"

She blew out a breath. "No. But I searched his bag while

he was sleeping. Unless he's hidden some in the lining of something, he doesn't have any more drugs with him. Which means he'll want to leave soon to score some more. Hopefully by tonight or tomorrow."

"You can't just make yourself kick him out?"

"He pleaded for one more day. I figure I could give him that, but then I really will boot him out the door."

"Okay. Stay safe, sweetheart."

"You, too, Brice." She leaned up to kiss his hand on the window, then walked to her car, giving him a wave as she drove off.

Brice started his truck and followed her to the library, parking with the engine idling until, shaking her head at him again, she gave him another wave before entering the building. Finally assured she would be safe, he headed off to get coffee, grab something to eat, and check to make sure his brothers hadn't changed their minds about doing the bank meeting without him.

Then he'd pay a call on the town sheriff and call in a favor. He might have had to restrain himself last night, but this threat to Mary's safety and well-being was going to be eliminated today.

TWO HOURS LATER, Brice parked his truck a street away from Mary's cottage and walked toward her backyard. After slipping through the greenery that separated her yard from the neighbor on the other side, he silently made a circuit of her cottage, looking and listening intently. After ten minutes of observation, he determined that her brother was in the kitchen where, from the sound of it, he was making himself coffee.

Entering unannounced could get him shot, if her brother was packing, but Brice hadn't gotten the impression that he was. Still, it was a risk—but he didn't want to give the man advance notice to flee or barricade himself in a room somewhere.

Looking at the front door, he shook his head. If Mary intended to buy this house, he really needed to get her a better security system than that old turn-button door and a bolt lock. Quickly, he inserted the tool that pushed back the bolt, released the mechanism, and walked in.

"Making me some coffee?" he asked, watching Joey intently, ready to duck and roll if the man went for something at his waistband or pocket. But, looking strung out and nervous, Joey just said, "What are you doing here?"

"Could ask you the same question. You're supposed to be gone."

"What business is it of yours? Maria's my sister. I have a right to visit her if I want."

"You don't have the right to interfere in her life or put her at risk. What if whatever lowlife you offended enough to make you run finds you in her house? Do you want to be responsible for getting her shot—again?"

Joey flinched. "That wasn't my fault."

"Maybe not. But I'm not prepared to risk having it happen again. After you drink that coffee, you're going to get in that rental car parked a block away, drive out of Whiskey River, and never come back."

"Who are you to tell me what to do? It's a free country."

"For law-abiding citizens, yes. Maybe not for Joseph A. Giordano. Convicted of two juvenile offenses, with community service as your punishment. As an adult, arrested twice on possession charges, remanded into a treatment program. Suspect in a shooting in L.A. a week ago."

"I had nothing to do with that! I was just a bystander."

"Tell it to the judge. There are arrest warrants out in the case. By rights, I should cuff you and take you in now. But because you're Mary's brother, I'll give you half an hour before I report to the local police that I saw a suspicious person skulking around Mary's house, who then drove away in a dark-blue rental car, though I only caught three of the numbers on the license plate. By the time they can trace that, you can be halfway to the woods around Caddo Lake if you keep to the back roads. Where you go from there, I don't care, as long as you never come back to Mary's. So, do I escort you to the sheriff's office now, or do you leave town voluntarily?"

Joey stared at him, his hands shaking. Definitely coming down off something, Brice thought. All the more reason to get him out of Mary's house immediately, and for good. "Don't give me much choice, do you?"

"That was the idea."

"Okay. Let me drink my coffee and get my bag, and I'll go."

"I'll get the bag. You drink the coffee." On the off chance that her brother might have a weapon stashed in it, Brice didn't want him to be the one fetching it.

He walked down the hallway and into the guest bedroom, then picked up the leather overnight bag sitting beside the bed. A quick examination confirmed there were no weapons in it, thankfully. Mary's brother was definitely not the muscle in her uncle's organization.

He carried the bag back to the kitchen and stood, arms crossed, until Joey, looking surly and increasingly agitated, finished the coffee. Then pointed to the door. "Out. Now."

Joey threw him a furious look. "Always have hated cops."

"You're breaking my heart."

Brice kept a laser-focused gaze on the man while he picked up his bag and walked to the front door. Then followed him down the street until he got into his rental car and drove off.

Now to go see Mary and let her know the cause of her anxiety had just left town.

Catching a glimpse of himself in his rearview mirror after he parked outside the library, Brice rubbed the scruff of whiskers on his chin, thinking he really ought to go back to the ranch, shower and shave. But disreputable as he looked, he was too impatient to reassure Mary, see the stress and worry fade from her face, to waste time cleaning up first.

Hopefully he wouldn't send Miss Shirley screaming in alarm when she saw him.

She did scan him up and down with a puzzled look, but replied cordially to his greeting and confirmed that Mary was in the reference room. He strode down the hallway, but stopped short on the threshold, savoring his first glimpse of her as she sat at the reference desk, her attention on her computer screen.

Since she'd started seeing him, she'd stopped wearing the ugly bag dresses. The summery, flowered-print sundress she wore today showed her bare shoulders, while her long, curly dark hair was pulled to one side with a clip. She wore only a dusting of powder and a little eye makeup that accentuated those fascinating dark eyes.

Warmth and tenderness swelled his chest. He couldn't wait to have that serious talk about the future . . . and start making plans to make her his forever.

Apparently sensing someone's presence, she looked up. "Brice! What are you doing here?" Her smile of welcome fading, she said anxiously, "Has something happened?"

"Everything's fine," he soothed, coming over to give her a kiss. "I just wanted you to know that your little familial problem has been resolved."

"Resolved? How, resolved?"

"I stopped by to visit with your brother this morning. Convinced him that it would be in his best interests to leave immediately."

She looked at him suspiciously. "You must have been pretty persuasive."

"As he represented a potential danger to the community, before I went to see him, I felt justified in accessing the national criminal databases. Saw the juvenile offenses and the drug convictions. And there was a shooting in L.A. last week, involving members of the Giordano organization."

"A shooting!" Mary cried. "Joey carries things for Uncle Sal, but I can't believe he'd be involved in a shooting."

Brice nodded. "He insisted he had nothing to do with it. I told him there had been arrest warrants issued in the case, and because he was your brother and 'family,' gave him half an hour to leave before I contacted police—or if he refused to leave, I would take him in immediately. I don't think he wanted to tangle with me. So he left."

Mary swallowed hard. "Thank you, Brice, for not arresting him. But . . . isn't that illegal? Couldn't you get in trouble as, I don't know, an accessory abetting the escape of a wanted man?"

Brice shook his head. "There were arrest warrants issued—but none of them were for him. He just assumed one was, and I didn't correct his assumption. The threat of believing he's wanted should keep him on the move, though. As long as he ends up far away from you, I'll be happy."

Mary wrinkled her nose. "That sounds . . . like skating pretty close to the edge of what is permissible."

"Close, maybe. But not over. Sometimes I have to make that call, balance the right of an individual to privacy with the need to protect the community. Protection always trumps privacy in my book. Like with you, when I needed to know you were no threat to Bunny."

Her eyes widened and her jaw dropped. "When you needed to know about me?" she echoed. "Are you saying . . . you investigated *me*?"

Too late, Brice realized what his overtired brain had let him blunder into saying. He'd never told Mary about his snooping, which was probably a mistake. He should have confessed it long ago. To be honest, though, once his fears had been relieved, he'd forgotten about it.

Bad call. Because right now, Mary looked indignant.

"I hope you were duly gratified to discover I wasn't wanted for anything!" she said angrily. "And that I had never been accused or convicted of a crime. What gave you the right to investigate me? Can you just . . . look up anyone you want, anytime you want? Aren't there procedures now that limit stuff like that?"

"There's usually a review," he admitted.

"Which you chose to omit. Thank you, Texas Ranger, for violating my privacy." She shook her head. "I don't believe this. It's like my father all over again. Nobody in this town would have had any reason to suspect me of anything. I go to work, do my job, don't bother anyone. But that's not enough to protect me from the suspicions of the law, is it? Just like it was never enough for the police who harassed Papa all his life. And when they couldn't find anything, they called out the IRS agents, who audited his business every single year. Every. Single. Year. Despite never finding any records out of order, much less any evidence of criminal activity. I thought you were different. I guess I was wrong."

"Wait a minute," he protested, as angry as she was now. "It's not like I impugned your reputation before the whole town! I really didn't think I would find anything when I checked, but good grief, Mary, remember how much time you spend with Bunny! Nobody knew much of anything about you, where you came from, what you'd done before you came to Whiskey River. I just wasn't comfortable trusting only my instinct that someone who was that much of a mystery didn't pose a danger to her."

"Since if I'm unknown, I must obviously be an escaped criminal. I moved halfway across the country to escape being Uncle Sal's little princess, and still I get investigated."

"That's really not fair, when I had no way of knowing—"

"Enough!" she said, cutting him off. "I hardly slept all night, I'm exhausted and worried, and I can't deal with this. Leave, please."

He hadn't gotten any sleep either, which was probably why his stupid brain had let this slip. "I'll talk to you later when you're more reasonable."

"Oh, yes, because I'm the unreasonable one. Merely angry at having my privacy grossly invaded because you have the power to do it, and you could get away with it. Just like all the police who harassed Papa back in L.A." She shook her head, fury clear in her eyes. "A *Texas Ranger*. Joey was right. I was an idiot. Goodbye, Brice."

She jumped up, shoved her chair in, and stalked back to a door marked "Private—Library Staff Only." Walking quickly through, she closed it behind her. He heard the click of a lock.

Angry, exasperated, and annoyed with himself, Brice hesitated, but after a moment, turned and walked out. He wasn't about to pound on the door and demand that she come out and talk. It probably wouldn't accomplish very much to continue the conversation now anyway. They were both overtired, stressed, and not thinking clearly.

Setting his jaw, he walked back out to his truck and set off for the ranch.

Chapter Fourteen

IN THE MORNING, a week later, Brice paced his condo in Austin. After their argument at the library, he'd texted Mary from the ranch and proposed they meet again to sort things out.

She'd replied that it might be better for them to take a break and not see each other for a while. Upset and angry, he'd replied *whatever you want,* and after dinner—and no more texts from Mary—had driven back to Austin.

Even the news delivered over dinner that night by his triumphant brothers that their confrontation with the bank had led to the president backing down and restoring the original loan terms hadn't been able to cheer him. They probably suspected something was wrong when he wasn't able to join wholeheartedly in their celebration over surviving this latest threat to the Triple A.

He passed it off as worry over the upcoming operation to apprehend the suspect in his ongoing investigation. He didn't think they believed him, but they were wise enough not to press him about it.

Over the past week, he'd texted her several times asking

how she was. She'd replied saying she was fine—but not suggesting she was ready to see him again.

He took another sip of his strong coffee, but that just reminded him of Mary and her espresso and biscotti. Putting down his cup, he walked out onto his balcony overlooking the Austin skyline.

He'd thought she was The One. Heck, he'd been on the point of proposing the next time he saw her. He couldn't believe she'd let one stupid argument derail what had been so good for both of them. Not that he blamed her for getting angry, but once she cooled down, how could she continue to blame him for wanting to make sure Bunny was safe?

Maybe it was time to give up on the idea of one special woman and go back to playing the field.

Even though that option didn't sound very appealing.

Irritation faded to depression, the result of the hurt and the ache of longing he'd felt ever since leaving her behind that closed door in the library. Besides, over the last week, as he cooled down and finally tried to look at the argument from her viewpoint, he better understood why she'd gotten so upset.

After having grown up witnessing the constant scrutiny to which her law-abiding father had been subjected, both she and him saddled with reputations solely because of their kinship to a criminal, she couldn't help but be sensitive to the idea of being investigated when she'd done nothing to warrant it. Her opinion of the police could hardly have been improved when they hadn't found or prosecuted the shooters who had killed her fiancé and her baby and put her in the hospital for weeks.

And, he thought, squirming a little uncomfortably, she did have a point. He hadn't followed procedures when he tried to trace her, rationalizing that if he found nothing, no one needed to know he'd ever looked, and if he did find something, then he would go through channels to make the investigation official. He had taken advantage of his power and authority, even if he'd done it for a very good reason.

Maybe he should do a better job of trying to apologize.

Because he realized it wasn't just that the idea of dating a variety of women didn't appeal. There was only one he wanted. Sometime between their frosty first meeting in the library and watching her childlike delight at walking through the display gardens at that Hill Country nursery, he'd fallen off the swinging bachelor train. He neither could nor wanted to climb back on.

Like it or not, he loved Mary Williams Maria Giordano. And he needed to do whatever was necessary to recover from his false step and win her back.

A slow burn of determination, fueled by hope and excitement, lifted his dull spirits. Good thing he'd been keeping a mental list of her favorite things.

LATER THAT AFTERNOON, Mary sat at her computer reviewing files. When not needed to assist library patrons or do other routine work, she'd been reading through old texts and documents, typing the text by hand into a database so that all the rare books, many of them too fragile to scan, could be added in digital form to their collections.

It was tedious work that required a lot of concentration to complete the transcription accurately. Which was a good thing. She needed to keep her mind occupied, lest it drift back to her ugly argument with Brice.

At first, hurting and feeling betrayed, she'd been sure that breaking with him was unavoidable. What was crime boss niece Maria Giordano thinking, to get involved with an officer of the law? She'd run all the way to Whiskey River and still been subjected to scrutiny, just as if she'd never left L.A.

But as the week dragged on, as her anger faded and she began to realize how huge a part of her life Brice had become, she started having second thoughts. With her inbred aversion to lawmen, she'd tried to block out of her mind what he did for a living. Since he pursued his cases elsewhere, seldom ever appearing in Whiskey River badged up and working, she'd been able to avoid thinking of him as a law enforcement officer. But if they were to have a future, she needed to face that fact squarely and decide if it were, in fact, possible for Maria Giordano to let go of her innate prejudice against what he did and accept him fully, as a man and a lawman.

Except for that one instance when he investigated her, she had no other indication that he'd ever used his position to intimidate or coerce anyone, or to gain some advantage. And if she were really honest, had their situations been reversed, to make sure Bunny wasn't in danger, she would have been tempted to do the same thing he had.

Could she reconcile herself to loving a lawman?

Realizing she'd once again lost her place in the document, with a huff of frustration, she was scanning the page, trying to find where she'd left off reading, when the door to the reference room opened with a rush of cool air. She looked up to see Miss Shirley walking toward her, a huge smile on her face and a large vase of long-stem roses in her hand.

"Somebody has an admirer," Shirley said, beaming. "I'm so pleased for you! Especially if they're from who I think they are." She set them down on Mary's desk and waved a hand. "Not that I'm asking—it's your business. I didn't even peek at the card!"

Laughing, Mary said, "I appreciate that. Thanks for bringing them in."

Shirley lingered another minute, obviously hoping Mary would open the card and reveal the identity of her sender. But when Mary made no move to take it from the holder, not wanting to read the message until she was alone, with no one to view her reaction, Shirley said, "You enjoy them, now," and walked back out.

They probably were from Brice. She couldn't imagine who else would send her flowers. Her breath catching in her throat in both thrill and dread, she pulled out the card and opened it.

> *Red for beauty. Red for passion. Red for the brilliance you bring to my life. I'm sorry we argued. Can we start again? Brice.*

She breathed in the deep rose fragrance, letting her finger trace the edge of one velvet petal. She wouldn't minimize the gulf she'd have to cross to fully accept Brice. Without question, his job and his deep sense of commitment to protect his fellow citizens were an essential part of who he was.

He wouldn't want to give that up. She couldn't ask him to.

But when she thought of him, the deep joy she felt being with him, she knew she had to make the effort. To fully become Mary Williams and leave the griefs and prejudices of Maria Giordano behind.

He'd asked for a chance to start again. She could at least promise that.

Picking up her phone, she texted, *Got the beautiful flowers. Thanks. Maybe we do need to talk again.*

After breathing deeply of the roses' sweet aroma, she went back to typing, only to have her phone ping with a text almost immediately. As if he'd been waiting for her to get the flowers and know what her response was.

Great. Wrapping up an operation this week, not sure when I'll be done. I'll text you. Can't wait to see you again.

She smiled, feeling her spirits lift. Brice McAllister might wear a Ranger's star, but he was also the strong, compassionate man who'd held her when she wept over the loss of her child. The encourager who'd advised her to find out for sure whether the doctors' predictions that her injury would prevent her from carrying a child were still valid. A kind man, infinitely patient with the glacial pace of her slow turn from isolation back to embracing life. And despite his obvious desire, he'd never pressed her for the physical intimacy for which they both burned.

Claiming a man like that was worth getting past a lifetime of hurts.

After work, Mary brought the flowers from the library, wanting to smell their wonderful fragrance throughout her house. As she set them on the island, she remembered with a shudder how her brother had forced his way into her home.

How skillfully Brice had disposed of her problem! Leading her brother to believe, without actually telling him a lie, that he was a wanted man. Even though, with Joey admitting he'd been associated with the shooting, Brice could have taken him in for questioning as a potential witness.

He hadn't, because of her.

She had to admit, when it came right down to it, she

wasn't sure she would have been as successful at getting Joey to go. He'd survived his shady career thus far by exercising his highly developed instinct for self-preservation. She didn't have the muscle to have physically thrown him out if he'd refused to leave. Her only other recourse would have been to call the local police, and he'd known she would never do that.

The longer he stayed, the greater the danger that Bunny would come to check on her. Or, coming down from the high of whatever he'd been taking, that Joey would sneak out to try to score more drugs and be caught or injured, leading police back to her.

Her heart ached again, as it did whenever she thought of her baby brother. He'd been such an engaging, funny, active, loving little boy. Much as it hurt to send him away, especially knowing he was in trouble, there was nothing she could do for him now. Nothing but protect her new life and the people in it that she cared about.

She'd changed into casual at-home attire when she heard a knock at the back door. Despite knowing it was unlikely to be Brice, a surge of excitement went through her. But when she hurried to open it, Bunny stood on the doorstep. Holding out a bunch of flowers.

"Mommy said Uncle Brice texted her and asked her to have me bring you some roses from the garden. These deep-pink ones with the yellow centers that are your favorites."

After debating whether or not to ask, she said, "Did he

say why?"

"Mommy said because he wanted you to be happy, and he knows these flowers make you happy."

"They do. They are beautiful. Thank you for bringing them."

"Mommy says when someone hurts your feelings, you need to give them a chance to say they're sorry, and forgive them."

Had Brice said something to Elaine? Probably not, she concluded. His message—and the fact that he hadn't been to see her in more than a week, would probably have led Elaine to suspect something had gone wrong between them. "Your mommy is right."

"So you aren't going to stay mad at Uncle Brice, are you?"

"What makes you think I'm mad at Uncle Brice?"

"Because he used to visit a lot and I haven't seen him in forever. And because you come out in the garden and look really sad and stare at the same plant for a long time without picking anything. Every once in a while he teases me too much and I get mad. Then he always says he's sorry, and I forgive him."

"That's very good of you."

"Not really. I could never stay mad at Uncle Brice. I love him too much and I would miss him if he didn't come see me. You'll forgive him, too, won't you? Cause I really do love cooking and gardening and going for rides with both of you. Please? I promised Mommy I wouldn't ask to come over all the time and be a pest."

Looking into the little girl's earnest eyes, Mary's heart melted. "You are never a pest, *mimmo*. We love being with you too."

She nodded. "Good. Because I think Uncle Brice would be really sad if you didn't forgive him. I know I would be, if I hurt your feelings or made you mad. And I don't like Uncle Brice to be sad."

"We'll just have to do something about that, won't we, then?" Mary said, smiling.

"So you'll ask him to come over and make dinner with us?"

"We'll see. He texted me that he was going to be working out of town for a while and he'd let me know when he was finished."

"Good!" Bunny said, clapping her hands. "We can make a really special dinner. Then you'll both be happy again."

A child's world was so simple, Mary thought, giving the little girl a hug. A few flowers, a few words of apology, a good dinner, and all would be well again.

It wouldn't be nearly as easy as that. But she was determined to try.

MARY WAITED A few more days, hoping to get the text from

Brice saying he'd wrapped up his case and letting her know when he'd be coming to Whiskey River. Although she waited in vain for that, he sent several other things.

A package from the local bookstore with a volume on Texas legends and proverbs he'd mentioned being his brother's favorite, with a note that said, "My favorite way to encounter Texas proverbs is to hear you say them."

A selection of small-potted herbs in a tray to set under her kitchen window, sent from the native plant nursery they'd visited. The card included with them read, "A spicy reminder of our visit here. Hope to make many more."

Finally, after four days exchanging several texts a day with no mention of his return, making it now almost two weeks since she'd seen last him, after getting home from work, she abandoned the last of her reserve and texted, *Missing you. When do you think you'll be back?*

She carried her phone with her into the garden while she picked tomatoes and basil for caprese, then set everything on the kitchen island while she sliced the cheese, assembled the salad, and added the balsamic vinegar. Checking in case she'd somehow missed hearing the ping of a reply, she looked again before she started to prepare the rest of dinner, but nothing yet.

Normally, he responded quickly to a text, but he was working a case. He might be too occupied to be able to reply. But after she'd put the salmon and potatoes into the oven to roast, she texted him again.

By the time she finished her meal and sat at the table, sipping her glass of wine, she was starting to worry.

It was evening now, past time for Brice to be off work. Trying not to feel anxious but too agitated to sit still, she walked back into her garden, deadheaded some flowers, snipped a few herbs, and harvested another tomato for her lunch tomorrow. She checked her phone again; still no response.

Maybe he'd forgotten to recharge his phone and the battery had gone dead. But that wasn't likely, since he was technically always on call and would make sure he could be reached.

She looked up through the fading twilight to see Elaine and Tom come out on porch, carrying glasses of wine. And found herself walking over to them before she was conscious of what she was doing.

"It's a beautiful evening," Elaine said. "We just put Bunny to bed. Will you join us for a glass of wine?"

"Sure, I'd love it."

"Bunny tells me Brice has been sending you gifts," Tom said as he poured her a glass.

Elaine whacked her husband on his free hand. "You shouldn't ask her about that! What happens between them is private."

Tom held up a hand. "Hey, I'm not trying to interfere! Just to say that Brice McAllister is a good man, one of the best. If he's somehow done something boneheaded, I'd strongly urge you to give him a second chance."

Mary returned a strained smile. "We did have a . . . disagreement. But I think we'll manage to work it out."

"I'm so glad!" Elaine said, her expression delighted. "Bunny has been worried. Us too. None of us want Miss Mary and Uncle Brice to be unhappy if they could be so much happier together."

That reminder was enough to break through her restraint. "You—you haven't heard from him today, have you? I texted him hours ago, then a second time, and have had nothing back. Even when we were mad at each other, he responded pretty quickly to my texts."

To her further alarm, Elaine and Tom exchanged concerned glances. "How long has it been that you've not been able to establish any contact?" Tom asked.

"Hours."

While Elaine swallowed hard and reached over to take her husband's hand, Tom said, "I think you'd better call Duncan."

Even more worried now, Mary set her phone on speaker so Elaine and Tom could hear the conversation and dialed Duncan, who answered right away. "Mary, how are you?"

"Fine. Well, actually, I'm worried. I texted Brice several times today and he hasn't responded. I know he keeps his phone charged, and it's way past business hours now. I asked Tom Edgerton, who is here on speaker with me and Elaine, and he recommended I call you."

Duncan sighed. "Okay, this is confidential, but I expect Brice would want you to know. He texted me this morning saying he expected to have his case wrapped up today and would be at the ranch for dinner. Around midafternoon, one of his team called. The suspect they went out to apprehend turned violent, holing himself up in his house with a shotgun. It was a bank fraud case, and apparently the guy they are going to arrest is a prominent man in the financial community. An arrest and conviction will destroy his reputation, and even after he serves his prison time, his life will be ruined."

"Should have thought of that before he started committing fraud," Tom muttered.

"Exactly," Duncan said dryly. "Now it's an active-shooter incident, which means Brice would have been called in even if he weren't already working the case."

Terror went through Mary as she heard again the screech of a car's tires braking beside her car, the blast of a handgun, the windshield shattering glass over her. The shock of the pain and the blood . . .

"Why . . . why would Brice be there?" she asked, struggling to banish the memories.

"He's the sharpshooter on the SWAT team. Didn't you know?"

Dimly, Mary remembered Elaine and Brice talking about Brice's position. Not wanting to envision him as a police officer, she'd deliberately blocked out that part of the conversation.

"So . . . he might get shot?" she asked, the possibility sending another stab of fear through her. Brice . . . lying on the ground, blood pooling on his shirt . . .

"There's a negotiator there now. They'll try to talk the guy down, get him to lay down his weapon and give himself up. Brice is a sharpshooter; he won't storm the building, if it comes to that. His job is to take up a position where he can watch the exit points and take down the perpetrator if he threatens to shoot the negotiator or any of the other officers. Or to try to wound or disarm the suspect, if he can, if the man tries to shoot himself."

"But he could be shot."

The phone went silent for a minute. "There's always a chance something bad could happen. People are unpredictable. He lost a good friend, a highway patrolman, who was doing a routine traffic stop. Danger's always out there."

"When will you know something?"

"He'll let us know as soon as the situation is resolved. If you've texted him, I'm sure he'll text you back too."

"When do you think that might be?"

There was another silence. "No idea. It really depends on the suspect."

"Okay. Thanks for letting us know, Duncan. We won't say anything to anyone."

"Please don't. But don't worry, Mary. These units train together all the time, and Brice is very, very good at what he does. I'll talk to you later, okay?"

"Thanks," she said again, punching off the call. But she didn't feel much better. A bullet on a killing trajectory didn't divert because of training or expertise. If it were coming straight at you, it would still be lethal.

"Shall I make some coffee? It might be a long night," Elaine said.

"You don't need to babysit me," Mary said. "And I didn't mean to intrude on your evening. I can wait at home."

"Hey, we're as concerned as you are," Tom said, patting her hand. "Having you stay here would be selfish, really. We know you'll be one of the first people Brice texts once the team stands down."

"If you're sure . . ." She really didn't want to be alone just now. She'd had a hard enough time trying to wrap her head around him being a lawman. She'd resisted even thinking about the implications so effectively that until now, she'd never even considered how often he must be in harm's way.

Did she really want to turn her heart over to someone who might end up bleeding to death at her feet, as Ian had?

She wouldn't think about that. She'd just concentrate on thinking of him tired, weary, and ready to come home and shower up after the long standoff was successfully concluded.

She only hoped the negotiator was as good at his job as Duncan said Brice was at his.

Chapter Fifteen

GLANCING AT THE clock for the umpteenth time, Mary noted that it was after midnight. Elaine had fallen into an uneasy sleep on the couch, her head on Tom's shoulder. Fueled by worry, adrenaline and strong coffee, Mary was not able to doze. She paced the back terrace, trying to keep from thinking of Ian's body jolting as the bullets struck.

Brice was a pro, Duncan had said. The SWAT teams drill and drill to perfect every movement, every type of infiltration, Tom had assured her. Brice wouldn't go in with the storming unit anyway; he'd be positioned in an observation post where he could provide cover.

But none of those reassuring words could lessen the sense of dread that sat like a giant bolder in her belly.

When the ping of a text finally came, sometime after one o'clock in the morning, she jumped a foot. Her fingers trembling so could hardly swipe the phone, she saw the text and clicked on it. *Op finished. Everyone safe. Sorry you were worried. Talk to you tomorrow.*

She sagged into a chair, weak with relief, letting the tears spill over for a minute before she went over to gently shake

Tom and Elaine on the shoulder. Rousing immediately, Tom said, "What did you hear?"

"He's safe. It's over. He'll be back in Whiskey River tomorrow."

"Praise God," Elaine whispered, hugging her husband.

"Thanks for staying here and letting us know," Tom said. "You're welcome to crash in the guest room."

"No, I think I can make the walk back to my own bed," Mary said. "Thanks for the offer, though."

Elaine rose and gave her a hug, then she and her husband walked Mary out to the back porch. "We'll stay here and watch until you're safely inside," Elaine said. "Give us a wave after you've turned on the lights and checked that everything is okay."

Now that there were no fugitive brothers hiding within, she was pretty sure her house would be safe. "I will. Thanks again for keeping vigil with me."

"Our pleasure. Brice is dear to us too. Get some sleep, now," Elaine said.

"Good night," she said, then walked down the stairs, crossed the moonlit yard and went back into her cottage. After doing a quick check of all the rooms, she walked back to her porch and waved the "all clear."

They gave her a wave in return, then turned to go back into their house.

Too tired to shower, Mary threw on her T-shirt and jammie bottoms and climbed into bed. But she didn't sleep well.

The bad dreams about the incident in L.A. that she'd not had for months returned every time she dozed off. She awoke each time gasping for air, paralyzed with fear, until her brain managed to right itself and return her to the present.

If she moved forward with Brice, would she invite a lifetime of these? It had been hard enough to envision overcoming a lifetime of resentment and suspicion. Worse than the prospect of recurring dreams like these, could she risk loving a man she might lose again to violence?

Tomorrow, Brice would be coming to see her again. She had no idea what she was going to tell him.

Chapter Sixteen

AROUND NOON THE next day, Mary got the text she'd been expecting. *Stop by after work? Think we need to talk.*

They did. If only she knew for sure what she was going to say. Still, delaying was unlikely to make her muddled mind clearer. Blowing out a deep breath, she texted back, *Meet me at the cottage.*

Good thing the library wasn't busy. She was able to sit over her computer the entire afternoon, supposedly transcribing another rare text. She'd be lucky if she'd typed even a chapter before closing time arrived and she shut down the machine. As she walked past the head librarian's desk, Shirley lifted her eyebrows, to which Mary replied with bland smile, unwilling to give a verbal response about her plans. With a sigh, Shirley said, "Have a nice evening, dear."

Her stomach was tied in knots so tight she could hardly get down a sip of water after she walked into her house. After texting Brice that she was home, ready for him anytime, she set up the espresso machine for coffee she wasn't sure she'd be able to drink, then paced around the room.

She was so *not* ready, two halves of her clashing for dominance. The safety, normalcy-craving part of her said that, wonderful as Brice was, she couldn't handle the uncertainty of loving a man who might be suddenly taken from her like Ian was. She couldn't handle the possibility that his job would give her nightmares like she'd had last night, night after night after night.

A diametrically opposed part of her, one that craved beauty and love and joy, insisted that accepting the risk and loving him was essential to her happiness. That if she turned him away, she'd be turning back to a life in which she was merely existing.

The ping of her phone made her jump. *Be right there,* Brice texted back.

Swallowing hard, she went back to pacing.

TEN MINUTES LATER, a mingling of panic and relief went through her as she heard Brice's truck pull up outside the cottage. A minute later came the knock at her door. Hands trembling, she walked over and opened it.

Brice stood on the threshold, gazing at her solemnly, a big bouquet of roses in his hand. Before she knew what she was doing, she flung herself at him, clinging to him, while he dumped the flowers and wrapped his arms around her, lifted and carried her back into the room, kicking the door shut behind him.

And then she was sobbing again, the fear and uncertainty and confusion robbing her of control. He hugged her back tightly, whispering "Shh, it's okay. With you in my arms again, everything's okay."

After a few minutes, she pulled herself back together and pushed away. "I was so scared," she admitted, gazing up into his face. "I was afraid I was going to lose you."

"No chance, sweetheart. I'm yours, all yours."

"Brice, I love you. I know I do. But I'm not sure . . . about a future."

"That's what we needed to talk about, right? So . . . let's talk."

Now that the moment had come, her thoughts still jumbled, she wanted to put it off. She hated herself for being so uncertain, terrified to move forward, unable to face sending him away. "Coffee?"

"Please."

She busied herself making it, hoping the familiar routine would settle her. Then brought the tray over to the coffee table, motioning him to the sofa and taking a seat beside him. "You first."

"Okay. I admit, I was . . . angry that you accused me of impropriety, then refused to listen to any explanation. For a few days, I thought maybe it would be a good idea to break things off. But once I calmed down and thought carefully about the kind of harassment your family had endured your whole life, I started to understand why you'd overreacted. It wasn't right, what the authorities did to your father. There have been abuses in the past. I can't do anything about that, but because we are given such power and authority, because the consequences of making a mistake can be catastrophic, we in law enforcement have to do better. And you were right, I had bent the rules."

He paused, sipping his coffee before continuing, "But more important, trying to envision returning to life as a bachelor just reinforced what I've known for a long time. I love you, Mary Williams . . . Maria Giordano. I want to be with you, only you. I want to protect you and love you for the rest of my life. I know my profession makes that . . . difficult for you. I suppose I could maybe look for some other line of work—"

"No." She held up a hand, halting him. "Your work is an essential part of who you are. Even I admit that, for the most part, it's valuable, lifesaving work. I couldn't ask you to give that up."

"You're sure? So you think you could try to adjust to it? I'd do pretty much anything for you, Mary. Even give up the Rangers, if you asked me."

"I've thought a lot about us too. Whether I could try to dismantle a lifetime of negative opinions about the police and truly start fresh. It won't be easy, but I think I can do that. But there's something harder."

"What?" he asked, taking her hand and kissing her fingertips. "Tell me, and I'll make it go away if I can."

"The shooter incident. Since I'd tried as much as possible to put out of my mind what you do, it never really struck me until last night that you go into harm's way. Brice, I still have nightmares about the attack. They came back again last night with a vengeance. Since they come on when I'm sleeping, I don't know how to fight against that."

Setting down his coffee cup, he drew her into his arms, and once again, she clung to him, able to stem the tears this time, but still shaking.

"I'm so sorry, sweetheart. I didn't know. Do you have the dreams often?"

Being in his arms, she felt so . . . safe. Protected. But his embrace couldn't protect her from the demons in the night. Demons the danger he worked with might revive all too often.

"At first, almost every night. Less and less as time went on. I hadn't had a really bad night since I came to Whiskey River—until last night. In the dreams, I'm in the car again, trapped, seeing the muzzle flash of the handgun, the windshield exploding, Ian jerking as the bullets hit. Blood . . . pain . . . then blackness."

He stroked her back. "Did you see a therapist after the attack?"

"No. I spent weeks recovering physically, then all my energy went to finding a school, moving out, finishing my studies. I didn't tell the doctors about the dreams. I didn't want to admit anything that would have given them an excuse to keep me in L.A. any longer than I needed to heal physically."

"The dreams sound like classic post-traumatic stress. The department recommends that we see a therapist any time there's an incident involving loss of life. Even when that possibility is part of your job, having it actually happen is traumatic. Even more so when it happens to someone who never expected to encounter violence. Seeing someone might help. It certainly couldn't hurt."

He released her, ran a gentle finger down her face. "I would never want to be responsible for trapping you in a relationship that brings you pain. But I don't want to let you go, either. I wish I could promise that I'd never be in danger again. But I can't. I *can* promise that we reduce the risk as much as possible. Training frequently over a variety of possible scenarios. When there is an incident, analyzing the area and strategizing the best way to approach and neutralize the target before ever setting foot on the scene. Since I'm not usually part of the team that goes in, if we have to go in, I'm at less risk than the others. But the risk is never zero. Does that make any difference?"

She sighed. "I don't know. Until yesterday, I never anticipated having the dreams come back. But I don't want them to destroy what we have either. I, too, thought long and hard about going back to living without you. But after the joy of sharing the last two months with you, I can't escape the fact that before I let you into my life, I was simply existing. Coming alive again means being vulnerable to pain, loss, risk—but also anticipation, excitement, joy . . . passion. I don't want to go back to living without those again. So . . . yes, I'd be ready to see a therapist. See if I can put those dreams back into the past where they belong."

"That means . . . you're willing to go forward with me?"

Pushing away the last of the fears that had held her back, she gave him a tremulous smile. "I think . . . I am. I want to embrace life, the future, and you. Forever."

He wrapped her in another hug, holding her tight, then kissed her passionately, a promise of his desire and devotion. When he broke the kiss at last, she laughed. "The last two weeks—Joey showing up, then then the active-shooter incident—pushed to the background what had been the most important news I'd been waiting to share. Remember I told you I had to go out of town on library business?"

"It wasn't library business."

"No. I had an appointment with an OB/GYN specialist in the Med Center in Houston. She'll have to do more testing, but she said there's a good possibility they have treatment options now that might enable to me to carry a child to viability. So I might be able to have a baby after all. She said if the tests proved that was not possible, she'd recommend a tubal ligation, but not to give up hope. So . . . either way, I'll be able to make love to you without fear."

"That's wonderful news!"

"The prospect of sharing my life with you, hopefully bearing your child . . . that's worth therapy and even bad dreams."

"You're sure?"

"I'm sure. I love you, Brice McAllister."

"I love you too, Mary Williams." He kissed her again, long, slow and tender. Then sat up, grinning. "I think I might just drop that harp through a cloud. Don't move—I've got something in the truck for you."

Jumping up from the couch, he loped out the door, then returned a minute later, box in hand. "For you. I didn't dare hope enough when I arrived to bring it in right away, but now's the time. Go ahead, open it."

Unwrapping the heavy box, she found inside the beautiful deep-blue Royal Lace Depression glass cookie jar she'd admired at Old Man Tessel's. "Brice, it's beautiful! Thank you."

"Look closer."

When she did, she noticed there was another small box inside the jar. After carefully setting aside the glass lid, she lifted out the box and opened it. Inside, a ring with a large center sapphire surrounded with diamonds winked up at her.

While she gasped, admiring it, Brice went down on one knee in front of her. "Will you marry me, Mary Williams . . . Maria Giordano?"

She held out her hand, letting him slip the ring on her finger. "With all my heart, Brice McAllister."

After giving him a joyful hug, she laughed. "After all, you're giving me back a single name. Forever in the future, I'll be just Mary McAllister."

ON A CRISP fall afternoon three weeks later, Brice stood with his brothers on the back porch of Tom Edgerton's house. The lawn had been set up in rows of chairs with an aisle down the middle, and garlands of flowers hung on the fences. The guests—his brothers' wives and children, Abby's husband's family, a few other close friends, and Miss Shirley from the library, were mingling about while Katie and Bunny, giggling with excitement in their flower girl dresses, were arranging rose petals in their baskets.

With Mary's permission, Brice had told his brothers about the trauma of her past, asking their help in reassuring her when he was called out with the SWAT team in future. Mary had agreed to his suggestion and contacted a mental health therapist the day after she accepted his proposal and had already attended several sessions, telling him she thought they were helping.

The sweetest part of the resolution for her, she'd told him, was his pressing her to invite her father to the wedding. For the first time in her new life, she'd be able to have a precious part of the old to carry her into the new.

Brice liked her father, though like his son, Mr. Giordano

chuckled at the idea of his daughter marrying a law officer. But he'd given them his blessing and promised to give away the bride.

Elaine scurried onto the porch. "Okay, everything's ready for the reception. The preacher's out back in the yard. I'm going to grab Tom and get in our chairs. He'll give you a nod when the preacher is ready for you three to walk out."

After Elaine rushed off, Duncan swiped a bottle of water from one of the reception tables and handed it to Brice. "Better take a drink. We'll need to be able to hear you when you recite your vows."

"I don't think I'll need it, but thanks." He was too sure that making Mary his wife was the smartest thing he'd ever done to be nervous.

"When are you going to start building that cottage down in the west pasture, by the creek, Brice?" Grant asked.

"Mary has six months to go on her lease in town, so we'll get started pretty soon. Might see if we can cut a trail from the site to the county road, so I can head back to Austin without having to drive all the way through Whiskey River."

"Still holding onto the condo in Austin?"

"Yes, I'll use it when I need to be in the city for a while. Might list it on a short-term rental site when I stay in Whiskey River. With all the festivals in Austin, the university events, the legislature, we'll have no problem getting rentals." He paused. "Mary's going to help me refurnish it."

Both brothers laughed. "The end of the sterile white box.

Woo-hoo," Grant said. "Sorta like your life. It was sterile and empty. Now you've got your own hot, talented, beautiful babe to make it worthwhile."

"I knew he was goner when he kept showing up in Whiskey River. That first month after he met Mary, he was here more than he'd been in the last two years put together," Duncan said.

"I was working on a case."

Both brothers rolled their eyes. "Yeah, work. A five-foot-seven, curly, black hair, beautiful, dark eyes-case," Grant said.

"The mighty oak fallen at last," Duncan added, making the *bauk-bauk-bauk* chicken noise.

"He just wised up," Grant said. "Being the youngest, it took him longer."

"Not that much longer," Brice retorted.

"True," Grant admitted. "Who could have imagined all three of us would get married within a year?"

"Who would have imagined when we went our separate ways after high school that we'd all end up back in Whiskey River?" Brice said.

Duncan looked at his brothers solemnly. "I think Daddy's smiling down on us today. It's what he always wanted, for the three of us to stay together on the Triple A." He raised his water glass. "To Daddy."

Grant raised his. "To Daddy and the Triple A."

Just then, there was a stir among the guests, like a breeze

rippling through the backyard as they all turned toward Mary's cottage. The flower girls walked from her garden into the backyard and started down the aisle between the chairs, tossing rose petals.

A minute later, Mary emerged from the cottage on her father's arm, and Brice caught his breath.

She looked radiant, her dark hair pulled back with a clip. Her long, lacy, white sleeveless dress swept the ground as she walked forward, her smile luminous as her gaze found his.

"The big moment's arrived," Duncan said, waving back to answer the signal Tom had sent him. Lifting his glass one more time, he said, "To Mary. The special lady who won my brother's heart, and to each of our special ladies."

"To our ladies," the brothers said.

Duncan gave Brice a brotherly shove. "Come on. Let's go get you married."

The End

Want more? Check out Duncan and Harrison's story in *The Rancher*!

Join Tule Publishing's newsletter for more great reads and weekly deals!

If you enjoyed *The Ranger*,
you'll love the other books in....

The McAllister Brothers series

Book 1: *The Rancher*

Book 2: *The Cowboy*

Book 3: *The Ranger*

Available now at your favorite online retailer!

More books by Julia Justiss

Scandal with the Rancher

A Texas Christmas Past

Available now at your favorite online retailer!

About the Author

After writing more than twenty-five novels and novellas set in the English Regency, award-winning historical author Julia Justiss expanded her focus to pen stories that take place on the frontier of the Texas Hill Country, near where she lives with her native-born Texas husband.

An avid reader who began jotting down plot ideas for Nancy Drew novels in her third grade spiral, Julia went on to write poetry and then speeches, sales promotion material and newsletters as a business journalist, before turning to fiction. Her awards include the Golden Heart for Regency from Romance Writers of America, The Golden Quill, and finals in Romantic Times Magazine's Best First Historical, the National Readers Choice, the Daphne du Maurier and All About Romance's Favorite Book of the Year.

Thank you for reading

The Ranger

If you enjoyed this book, you can find more from all our great authors at TulePublishing.com, or from your favorite online retailer.